RENEGADE *Hearts*

THE
★ KINNISON ★
LEGACY

BESTSELLING AUTHOR
AMANDA MCINTYRE

Dedication

You meet many different people in this industry and if you're lucky a select few become inspiration for the very heroes and heroines that you write about. When I think of as strong heroine, for example, I think of a capable woman, tenacious, determined, and maybe a bit sassy. Hope is the driving force in her life.

This book is dedicated to one such woman, Sharon Marion.

A sweet reader that I first met at a convention in New Orleans and who, in spite of incredible health obstacles, pushes on. You go, girl!

To all of those who struggle to carry on daily, despite the obstacles—believe in hope, believe that love will find a way, and it will be well.

~Amanda

Chapter One

"IT'S A GIRL!"

Dalton felt the testosterone level slip a little further from life, as he'd always known it. In what seemed a blur this past year, femininity had infiltrated the ranch once run by him and his brothers. First with Aimee capturing his brother Wyatt's heart, and then the discovery of their half-sister Liberty, who promptly sent Rein's world into a tailspin.

Now there was a new baby girl Kinnison to add to the mix. Still, nothing on earth made him happier than seeing the goofy look on his older brother's face. He pushed from the waiting room chair and grabbed Wyatt, his green scrubs splattered with blood, in a great bear hug. "Congratulations, old man. Who'd have ever thought you'd be a dad? Damn." He choked on the lump in his throat as he hugged Wyatt. The years when it had been just the two of them—struggling to survive, watching out for each other while their mom tried to find herself—whirled through his memory. The bond between them had been forged hard as steel, honed in fire.

An exhausted grin split Wyatt's unshaven face, weary-looking after the last twenty-four hours. "Aimee's tired. The baby was born feet first, Frank Breech they called it, but she's doing okay, too." He looked at Dalton. "I can't believe it's a girl. I can't believe how big she is. Almost nineteen inches long."

Dalton shook his head in disbelief. Since her first visit, they'd told the doctor they didn't want to know the gender. The doctor had leaned very much in favor of a boy, clearly, he was mistaken this round. The thought boggled his mind. "Do you have a name for her?"

Wyatt showed his million-dollar grin, the one that likely got Aimee and him into this predicament in the first place. "Grace June Kinnison. Gracie is what I'll call her."

"Gracie." It sounded right given all they'd been through over the past few months. "Gracie. I like it."

A tired but ecstatic Wyatt smacked him on the shoulder and pulled him in for another hug. "And God help us, you're Grace's uncle."

Uncle Dalton? Damn. Dalton's throat closed tight with emotion as he stepped away to allow the parade of well-wishers the chance to congratulate Wyatt.

"You named her Grace?" Betty, an old friend of the family, waited patiently, her arms ready to pull Wyatt into a fierce hug. "That's a beautiful name, honey. Oh, Jed would be so proud of y'all."

Dalton watched as Betty pulled Wyatt against her ample bust. She'd been like a mom, serving them and the community home-cooked meals at Betty's Café, End of the Line's only diner. His memory flashed to the joy his stepfather, Jed Kinnison, the man who'd adopted and raised three young boys as his own sons, would have had at this news. Perhaps this baby was God's way of saying that Jed's legacy should continue, despite his leaving this earth too soon.

The litany of well-wishers continued with Rein, Jed's true nephew who'd come to live with them after the accident that claimed Rein's parents. Liberty followed and after her, Michael and Rebecca Greyfeather, longtime friends of Jed Kinnison and the ranch.

Rebecca brought the new baby a handmade blanket. Dalton knew that given how much the community re-

vered his step-dad, the child would never want for anything. He considered it a miracle that the entire town of
End of the Line wasn't squeezed into the tiny Billings
waiting room.

A couple of months ago, Aimee's pregnancy had gone
awry after smoke inhalation caused her to go into pre-
mature labor. The fire, set on the main ranch house, was
intended as revenge from Liberty's former employer and
ex-boyfriend.

Though the fire destroyed much of the back of the
house, there was still extensive repair and remodeling that
was required before anyone could live in it. As a precau-
tion, doctors placed Aimee on complete bed rest for the
duration of the pregnancy, and she and Wyatt moved into
one of the guest cabins until the work was completed.

"Mr. Kinnison?"

Dalton felt a tug on his leg and he looked down to
find little Emilee Juarez, Michael and Rebecca's great-
niece. She'd come to live with her aunt and uncle at
the tender age of three, but referred to them as grandma
and grandpa. No one said much about the transition, or
why Angelique hadn't returned with her. But most folks
in the little town were accepting of such things. God
knows they'd accepted Wyatt and Dalton as Jed's sons after their mother had married Jed, then abandoned them
on Christmas day.

"You want to know a secret?"

"What's that, darlin'?" Dalton squatted down to look
into her dancing eyes.

She grinned, barely able to contain her excitement.
The child's infectious delight prompted his smile.

"I'm going to help Miss Aimee with the baby after
she comes home. I think I'll make a very good babysitter,
don't you?"

He turned his ball cap backwards on his head and

tapped her little pug nose. For all of her seven years, he bet she kept Michael and Rebecca on their toes with those mysterious dark eyes and articulate speech. "That will be up to your mama and Ms. Aimee, I suspect."

Her brows rose into her bangs. "Oh, I know I will be helping. I've seen it."

Dalton hid his surprise at her adult response. He had little—make that *no*—experience with kids, but remembered himself at that age and figured kids saw things the way they wanted. Then again, he'd heard Michael talk before about Emilee's uncanny way of predicting things. He claimed her Crow lineage gave her these powers and that Emilee's came from a long line of "seers" on his mother's side.

"Ok, punkin', but you best talk it over with your Aunt Rebecca."

"You mean my *grandma*?" she corrected him with another crook of her brow.

Dalton hesitated, startled how quickly the female persuasion learned to use the silent gesture as a symbol of defiance. "Of course," he said, silently chiding himself for the faux pas. "Grandma Rebecca."

"Emilee," a soft but stern voice issued behind Dalton.

He stood and awkwardly patted the top of the little girl's head.

"Stop pestering Mr. Kinnison."

"No harm done—" His brain stopped as did his words when he stood to face Emilee's mother, Angelique Juarez. He hadn't seen much of her since Wyatt and Aimee's wedding. She'd started work at a veterinary clinic down in Billings, and while she and Emilee still lived with the Greyfeathers, she'd been busy most of the summer. Their brief encounter at the wedding hadn't gone well, and looking at her up close and personal sure as hell made him wonder why.

She was beautiful, perhaps more than he'd allowed himself to remember. He worked at ungluing his tongue from the roof of his mouth. "Uh…hi," he forced through his rattled thoughts. He blamed it on his lack of sleep— that, and being deprived of a *real* drink for the last twenty-four hours. His eyes, seemingly unaffected, couldn't stop staring at her. She wore a simple skirt that brushed her ankles topped with a soft, white low-cut top beneath a faded blue denim jacket. Pure country girl, from her long, dark braid, to her sun-kissed skin.

She bent down, those dark eyes admonishing her daughter. Fortunately, with her focus on Emilee, she didn't notice how he couldn't take his eyes off her.

"I'm not being a pest," the precocious seven-year-old answered with total vindication. "You don't find me a pest, do you, Mr. Kinnison?"

The little girl tugged on his shirtsleeve, jarring Dalton from letting his memories amble down the road of his past, to a night in a high school parking lot. It was a night he'd fought hard to forget, particularly after finding out she'd gotten married a few months later. He'd eventually gotten over the frustration, but he'd never fully gotten over the fact that she'd left out the fact that she was engaged. Seeing her again, her inclusion in the wedding was a landslide to everything he'd shoved into the attic of his mind. Did she remember?

Angelique rose and her gaze collided briefly with his. She hastily averted her eyes. "Come on, Emilee. It's time to get home and fix supper. The Kinnisons need some family time."

"But—"

Rebecca Greyfeather placed her hand on the young girl's shoulder. "You must listen to you mother, Emilee."

Across the room, Wyatt, with his head bowed slightly, allowed Michael to bless him and his new family. The gentle sound of Michael's poetic blessing, the wisdom in his voice, echoed in the waiting room full of now-silent visitors.

"It is an old ritual, meant to bless father and mother to be fruitful with many healthy children," Rebecca explained softly, as though she'd read his mind.

Emilee watched in rapt fascination, her hand curled in her grandmother's.

Angelique stood silently watching her Uncle Michael's ritual blessing. She stepped away, helping herself to a glass of water at the guest station.

"You apparently aren't into the ancient ways like your uncle?" Dalton walked to her side and helped himself to a glass of water.

She glanced at him. "My mother never spoke of the "ancient ways," as you call it." Turning back to the crowd, she effectively distanced herself. He was unsure if she meant for him to hear her mutter, "I doubt she'd have been able to remember much, anyway."

Dalton raised a brow and observed her body language as he downed his water, wishing it had a couple of ice cubes and a splash of Jack Daniels in it to ease the tension in his gut. It was no secret to her or anyone that he hadn't been as hospitable about her return as others in the town.

There was a lot he didn't understand about her. Aside from not telling him she was involved with someone else during the steamy encounter they'd shared at her five-year class reunion, she'd gone and left Emilee with her relatives while she stayed in Chicago. *That* he had a harder time understanding. Perhaps because he'd never gotten over the fact that his mom had abandoned him and Wyatt as teens, leaving them to be raised by a virtual stranger.

She pulled her shoulders straight, indicating to him that she'd only spoken to him out of politeness. Stepping forward, she took Emilee's hand, gently tugging her from Rebecca's grasp. "Come on, baby. Why don't we go down to the gift shop? Maybe we can find something to send up to Aimee and the new baby."

"Grace," Emilee said, beaming up at her mother. "They named her Grace, right, Grandma?" She shot a look toward the older woman. With Angelique working long hours, it appeared to Dalton that the lines of authority were still being worked out.

Angelique tossed her paper cup past him and hit the trash can squarely. "Congratulations, Dalton, on becoming an uncle."

Again, with the polite tone. She couldn't wait to get out of that room, away from him. He responded with a nod.

She shifted her purse to her shoulder and spoke briefly to her aunt before taking her daughter's hand and walking out without a backward glance.

Dalton looked at his feet and shook his head. He doubted that things would be any different between them even if he hadn't been an ass to her at Wyatt's and Aimee's wedding a few months back. He glanced up and met Rebecca's steady gaze. There were times he wasn't sure what Rebecca thought of him. While it seemed she was willing to speak to and help Wyatt and Rein, often bringing them special treats of homemade pies, she was standoffish toward him. He figured that it probably had something to do with whatever Angelique chose to tell her about that night before she returned to Chicago.

Dalton gave her a nod accompanied by an awkward smile, deciding he'd had enough of crowds today. Better that he put the past behind him and focus on today. This meant that, with any luck, there was a Cubs double-header showing on Dusty's new forty-seven-inch flat screen and a glass of Jack Daniels—neat—waiting for him. He found Rein and nudged him in the side. "I'm headed up to Dusty's." He glanced over at his half-sister Liberty, who was enthusiastically putting on a gown to go in to see her new niece.

"You sure you don't want to stick around and hold Gracie?" Rein asked, watching Liberty's enthusiasm.

"Nah," Dalton said, following his brother's smitten gaze. "There'll be plenty of time later. Aimee's folks are going to want to go in." He slapped Rein on the shoulder. "I'm guessing from that look in your eye that it won't be long before you guys are going to want to start going forth and multiplying."

Rein smiled at Dalton. "We've talked about it and both of us want a big family. But I've got a house to build first."

"We'll get things walled in before winter, that shouldn't be a problem. Is Liberty getting antsy to move out of the cabins?"

"Nah, she's had so much input on the decorating end of things that to her it's like home."

"But little room for expansion, right?"

Rein grinned. "Yeah, maybe. I think being around family has put some ideas into her head."

"Yeah, that's rough." Dalton loved Liberty like a sister who had been around for a long time. They actually had a lot in common, including her passion for playing pool. But he wasn't blind, and he knew from the torrid affair that she and Rein had that they belonged together.

Rein scratched the back of his neck, his face actually turning a shade of crimson.

Man, their lives were changing, and by the minute, it seemed—well, with the exception of him. He slapped his brother on the shoulder. "They will be amazing children and gorgeous, no doubt, because of Liberty," he joked.

Rein grinned and it quickly vanished as Dalton started to walk away. He touched his elbow.

"Hey, call if you need a ride, okay?"

Dalton offered a quick smile, having heard the line from both his brothers on an ever-increasing level. "Sure, I will."

"Mama?" Emilee spoke from the backseat where she was busy buckling her seat belt

"Yes, Em?" Angelique dug her sunglasses from her purse and tossed the bag beside her. She glanced in the back to check that Emilee's booster seat was correctly secured.

"Do you like Mr. Kinnison?"

The question gave Angelique pause, yet she was not surprised that her daughter had noticed how she'd tried to distance herself from Dalton Kinnison. Her daughter, she'd discovered, was a very observant little girl. Still, this wasn't a topic she wished to discuss with her. Being around Dalton from time to time was something she'd have to manage. With her internship as a veterinary assistant in Billings and with them temporarily living with her aunt and uncle, there were bound to be times when they would run into each other. Additionally, Emilee was already enrolled in the third grade at End of the Line elementary. Her life was here and Angelique didn't want to uproot her from the only family she'd known. Her daughter feeling safe and secure was priority. If that meant running into one of the Kinnisons, namely Dalton now and then, then that was something she'd just have to manage.

"Do you mean Wyatt? Of course—he and Aimee have been wonderful to all of us." She surmised her daughter spoke of another Kinnison.

"I meant Mr. Dalton."

"Ah." She paused briefly. "Well, the Kinnisons in general are a good family."

"You know, he called Grandma Rebecca my aunt."

"Well, perhaps Mr. Kinnison doesn't realize that you've always called them grandma and grandpa."

"Why?"

"Why doesn't he know?" She shrugged. "I suspect he has a number of other things on his mind. It's not something that too many people realize."

Emilee was silent and Angelique sensed the young girl assessing that information. She looked in the rearview mirror and found her daughter studying her.

"He just pretends to be mean, doesn't he?"

That stopped Angelique. Dalton Kinnison was perhaps reckless, arrogant, and drank too much, but he didn't have a mean bone in his body—finely honed as it was. She swallowed before she spoke, choosing her words carefully, her past with Dalton notwithstanding. "Emilee, it's not nice to say such things. He's never given you reason to believe he was anything but kind. Why would you say such a thing?"

"He always looks grumpy."

"Well, perhaps he has some issues that he is working out. That can make some people seem like they're grumpy."

"You mean that he drinks too much?"

She turned in her seat and pinned her daughter with a frown. "Where did you hear that?"

Emilee looked at her mother. "I heard someone say that he drinks too much at Miss Aimee's wedding."

"Young lady, it isn't polite to eavesdrop. Furthermore, you shouldn't believe everything you hear. It isn't polite or wise to go around repeating rumors. It could turn out very bad for everyone involved. Do I make myself clear?"

"So, I should wait until I know something is for sure true before I talk about it?"

Flabbergasted at her daughter's astute understanding—not to mention vocabulary—she started the car. "Let's make a deal. If you have any questions about anyone, why don't you come to me first, and we'll go from there? How's that?" She looked in the rearview mirror. "Meantime, I better not hear that you're spreading rumors about Mr. Kinnison or anyone else, for that matter."

"Mother, please." Emilee rolled her eyes.

Angelique shook her head. "Good heavens, when I was your age, I was still chasing butterflies and thinking boys had cooties."

"Boys *do* have cooties," she said falling into a fit of giggles.

Angelique's heart lifted as it always did hearing her daughter laugh. That's how childhood should be. There were days when she felt woefully inadequate as a mother. Her aunt and uncle had done an amazing job raising Emilee. Even now, after all the counseling help and the struggle to make it through night school to get a degree, she had moments where she wondered if she was qualified to be a mother.

"Mama?" Emilee held her stuffed pony on her lap. Angelique had sent it home the first Christmas after they'd taken Emilee back to End of the Line. Her heart squeezed every time she heard the word *mama* come from her daughter's lips. She'd missed so much; there was much to catch up on.

"Yes, Em?" She pulled out her sunglasses to guard against the brilliant late summer sunset as they drove the mountain road toward home.

"Do you think I could help with the horses this summer?" She plucked at the stuffed animal's tangled mane made of now faded yarn; some of the pieces had disappeared.

"I don't know Em, you might be pretty busy helping Grandma bake pies for Betty's Cafe." She glanced at her.

"I intend to help Aimee with the baby." Emilee's brows puckered. "When she's sleeping, then I could help with the ne—ne…. I can't remember the word that means people don't take care of their animals."

"Neglected horses?" Angelique prompted.

"Yep, that's what Grandpa said. He said they'll bring them to the ranch while they wait to get adopted."

She'd heard her aunt and uncle talking about the venture, but they hadn't mentioned anything specifically to her yet about helping. Ironically, it was her experience working with her uncle with his care for horses that ultimately prompted her finally to go from waitressing to getting a veterinarian assistant degree, hoping to one day follow in her uncle's footsteps.

"Grandpa said that maybe I could help him sometime. But he said I had to ask you first."

Angelique pulled into the old gravel drive of the three-story farmhouse where she'd spent a great deal of her childhood. So much time, in fact, that they'd created a room in the attic of the house for her—it had been her sanctuary, a place where she could daydream and be a kid, unlike the trailer where she was her mother's caretaker. Up there away from the world, she'd open the windows and listen to the sounds of the countryside at night and dream of better things.

She looked at the old front porch with its sagging front steps and splintered wood railing badly in need of paint. She thought of how many plans she'd made while rocking on that porch swing. "Unbuckle, baby girl, and come up here." She turned off the car, shifted to help her daughter over the seat, and settled her under her arm. Brushing back her daughter's dark braid—a miniature replica of her own —she smiled down at the little girl. "I'm very grateful that Uncle Michael and Aunt Rebecca were able to care for you when I couldn't."

Those dark amber eyes studied her, a steady look that sent a cold punch to her stomach and memories she dare not revisit. The fewer who knew about her past, the better for her and for Emilee. Not even her aunt had known the full scope of her lifestyle until Angelique's close brush with death. It had been the wake-up call that she'd needed to realize how out of control her life had become. How close she'd come to losing everything—including Emilee.

Angelique wrapped her arms around the little girl. She pressed her face against the top of her head, breathing in the scent of lemon shampoo and sunshine. Tears pricked at the back of her eyes. "When I was little Aunt Rebecca taught me to bake and sew. Uncle Michael used to give me books to read and taught me how to ride my first horse."

Emilee's eyes grew wide. "They've taught me those same things, mama. Aunt Rebecca even made me a special necklace for me to wear." She pulled it from beneath her pink hoodie. "See? She says it will keep the bad spirits away."

Angelique held the small talisman between her fingers, remembering one similar to it that she'd lost shortly after she and her mother moved to Chicago. Maybe if had she worn it, things would be different now....

She shook herself mentally. *What's done is done.* She smiled down at her daughter. At least she'd done one thing right. "You know, we don't have a choice about the family we're born into. I was lucky, as you've been, to have your aunt and uncle, and while they aren't my biological parents, I spent more time here as a child and think of them as parents. So, in a way, they really are your grandparents. Do you understand?"

Her tiny brows furrowed and then she nodded. "I do, and I like having a grandma and grandpa." She paused, turning her eyes to meet Angelique's. "But the best thing of all is having a mommy."

A tear escaped and slid down Angelique's cheek. There'd been moments over the past few years when she'd thought she'd never hear those words. She hugged her daughter close. "You are the best thing I've ever done, Emilee."

"But you're squeezing me too tight, mama." Her infectious giggle filled the car and Angelique's heart.

Sniffing back her emotion, Angelique opened the door and let her daughter scramble down from her lap. "Let's go get dinner started."

"And surprise Grandma and Grandpa," Emilee called over her shoulder as she ran up the front steps. She turned suddenly and pinned Angelique with twinkling eyes. "Mama, I like Mr. Dalton. Maybe you should try getting to know him and maybe you'll like him, too." Her daughter smiled then and trotted up the steps without a backward glance.

Angelique felt as though a ghost had visited her. There were times since she'd been back that her daughter would say or do things far beyond her years. Her uncle called it a gift. Her aunt would only shrug her shoulders.

A movement caught her eye and Angelique glanced up at one of the trees that shaded the house, one whose branches she could crawl onto from her bedroom window. Perched on one of the branches, partially hidden by brilliant green pine needles, sat a white owl looking down at her. It blinked once, hooted, and flew off, its wings spread majestically as it soared out of sight. She remembered some old Indian superstition about owls predicting impending storms and a chill ran through her. One of these days, the truth of her past would catch up to her and she would owe many an explanation—including her daughter.

Chapter Two

"BATTER UP! YOU'VE GOT TO give credit to that fine Iowa farm club down there in Des Moines for this guy. He's one of the youngest ever taken on by the Cubs and he seems to be showing great promise this year. Here's the pitch...."

A collective groan followed the few patrons seated around Dusty's bar on the late summer Saturday afternoon.

"Tough break." Concern tinged the announcer's voice. "This Cardinal pitcher is causing all kinds of heartbreak for Chicago fans here today at Busch stadium."

His co-host added to the bleak outlook of the game. "That's two strikes. It's the bottom of the ninth and the Cards are up by one. Just one to go and this will head into the history books."

Dalton pulled on the last dredges of his beer as he eyed the stats on the screen. He reached down on the stool beside him, picked up his tattered ball cap, the patch long since gone, and plopped it on his head. He'd clocked watching hundreds, maybe more, Cubs' games—even attended a game or two at Wrigley Field when he was in college and convinced himself that he loved the game. Truly, maybe he did. But deep down, tarnished by time, jaded by life, flickered an almost imperceptible hope of a wounded nine-year-old-boy—that by some miracle he'd be able to recognize his father. Hell, if that much of what she'd told him was even true. He snorted quietly, admonishing the notion. His mother hadn't exactly been the pillar of motherhood—not by a long shot. And when she left him, Wyatt, and their brand-new step dad, Jed Kinnison, on that fateful Christmas morning, all she left him was the Cubs ball cap and a note.

Dear Dalton,

You are the youngest, but I worry less about you than I do Wyatt. You've always had better 'street smarts' and for that reason I want you to keep an eye on him and take care of yourself—that much is important. The two of you will be better off in Jed's care. You may not understand that now, but one day I hope you'll see in your heart to forgive me and know that what I did was best for you boys.

I want you to have this ball cap. It belonged to your father, Dalton. I met him in Chicago and he was fresh from the farm club, sent up to play the big leagues. He was so handsome, strong, and determined, but he had a career and I wasn't ready to settle down in Chicago. He was a good man—young and on fire. I see the same in you that I saw in him, and that, along with Jed's teaching, makes me know you will be fine. Dream big, son, and remember to take care of yourself.

Love, Eloise

He shoved aside his thoughts, blaming it on his brother's recent leap to fatherhood.

"Need a fresh one...*Uncle Dalton?*" Dusty gave him a side grin as he leaned over the polished dark wood bar.

"He'll have one more," a familiar voice called from the entrance. "In fact, drinks for everyone. I'm a new dad!"

Cheers rose from the patrons and Dalton smiled as Wyatt, the man who rarely stepped into Dusty's bar, become the center of well-wishes and pats on the back. Some things deserved celebrating.

Rein walked in behind him and ushered Dalton over

to a booth. "How'd the Cubs do?" Rein held up four fingers to Dusty who nodded and sent over four cold brews.

"Not so great. Maybe next year." Dalton slid in across from him and followed Rein's gaze as they watched Wyatt.

Dalton hadn't seen Wyatt smile so much since the day he'd announced his engagement to Aimee. There'd been a few bets riding on that one, especially after the bout of jealously he'd displayed in public that led to a brawl between the Kinnison brothers and some good old boys. Damn, Aimee had been pissed. Dalton chuckled at the memory. Had it not been for her insistence that she and Wyatt hash out their differences that very night…well, let's say little Gracie might not have made it into the world.

Wyatt plopped into the booth beside Dalton. "I feel… amazing." He shook his head. "Man, you guys should have seen Aimee. The woman is incredible. I mean, to go through what she did for what? Almost eighteen hours straight?" He brushed his hands down his face.

"How long's it been since you had any sleep?" Rein asked.

Wyatt looked dazed. "I don't know, eighteen hours, at least. But I'm not tired."

Rein glanced at Dalton.

"You know; I honestly didn't think it would be a lot different than birthing a calf."

Dalton laughed aloud at Wyatt's reference. "You might not want to tell Aimee that, bro." He pointed a finger at his brother.

"I see the party is already started." Liberty smiled down at the three and scooted next to Rein, snuggling close under his proffered arm.

Wyatt, wrapped up in checking out pictures he'd taken, looked as though he was reliving each moment of the birth process. "God, will you look at this." He shoved the phone in Dalton's face.

"Jesus, Wyatt." Unable to avoid the picture, he stared at the wrinkled, purplish, infant covered with a cheesy white substance. "That's just sick, dude."

Wyatt tossed him a mischievous grin. "Yeah, I thought you'd like that." Oblivious, it seemed, to the rest of them, he went back to looking at his phone.

"You got any *after* the kid was cleaned up?" Dalton asked.

"Oh, here's one." He ignored his brother's request and showed Dalton the graphic photo. "It's me cutting the umbilical cord."

Dalton turned his face away and held up his hand. "I'm warning you."

"Man, I had no idea you were so squeamish." Wyatt studied him with a curious gaze.

Dalton shrugged. "I just don't understand the need for a play-by-play of this kid's birth."

Wyatt glanced at Rein and shrugged. "Yeah, you're probably right, but I want to document everything. I want her to know how important she was to us from the very beginning. Hell, Dalton, all we have is a few postcards of motels to show for our childhood. Nothing else, at least, until we met Jed." He took a sip of beer and sighed. "I want her to know where she came from and where she belongs."

"Can't argue with that." Dalton tapped his bottle to the others. This was his family and he needed to stop skulking around in the past. Being angry about how his mom abandoned them, about not knowing who his real dad—it was a lifetime ago. He knew he needed to let it go.

Liberty's chin quivered as she raised her beer and waited for the others to follow suit. "To making strong families who stick together and build something we can pass on to future generations."

"To family," he repeated. The toast had dissipated some of the tension rattling around inside him, righting his world a bit better.

"Speaking of legacies," Rein said. "I waited until after Gracie was born to let you know that we've got our first official tenant coming to stay at the cabins."

All eyes turned to Rein.

"Clay Saunders. He's a friend from college. You remember him, Dalton?"

"Guy with shoulders that look like granite?" Dalton answered. "Yeah, haven't heard from him in years. What's the story?"

Rein shrugged. "He enlisted after school, did a couple of tours in the Middle East. He was in a convoy taking supplies to a small town when his truck drove over an IED. He was lucky that he made it. None of the rest of his squad survived. Hank says he's struggled with being the only survivor." Rein glanced at his brothers.

"I can see how that'd be tough to deal with," Wyatt said

Rein continued. "He's been at Walter Reed, spent some time in a vet hospital in rehab, learning to walk again. Guess things have been rough for him the past few months. His marriage broke up, and he started having nightmares again."

Dalton listened, and remembered the hulk of a man he'd known in college. Played on the football team and at one time thought about a career in the pros. Suddenly Dalton's problems seemed puny by comparison. He blew out a sigh. "Man." He rolled his beer bottle between his fingers. "Sounds rough."

"Hank's been in touch with him and he called me the other day asking what I thought about Clay coming to spend some time here, maybe see how he could help out at the ranch."

Wyatt's brows pressed together. "What are his injuries? Is he able to walk, or are we talking a wheelchair? We haven't put in a paved walkway yet to the cabins. Honestly, with everything going on, that's been on the backburner."

Rein nodded. "That's why I wanted to talk to you first. He has a prosthetic leg that he's getting used to, but he also has a crutch and a motorized wheelchair. He's still getting used to everything. The guy used to be going all the time. Lately, Hank indicated it's hard to just get him away from the Xbox."

"Xbox isn't a bad thing," Dalton interjected.

"It is if it's your whole world."

Dalton nodded with a shrug.

Rein continued. "I think I'm pretty much up to code on our handicap accessible cabin, but I want Sally to stop by and check it over. I figure that if anyone would have any tips, Sally would after taking care of her dad in his house. A path would be nice, but I wasn't sure if it was feasible yet."

"Where is he living now?" Dalton asked.

"He's out in California with his sister and her family for a couple of weeks."

"It sounds like he just needs to find a purpose again. Feel useful. Actually, there's a lot he could do around the ranch," Liberty offered. "He could help with the horses. We have the cart. He could drive that around and maybe help haul supplies. Maybe he'd be receptive to learning some woodworking skills."

Rein nodded, a grin slowly curling his mouth. He planted a kiss on his wife's temple. "That is a brilliant idea, sweetheart."

"You think he'd be physically up to that kind of

work?" Wyatt asked, clearly erring on the side of caution. "Taking care of the horses could involve a lot of standing, maybe even riding. Has he ever ridden a horse?"

"The Clay I used to know would never walk away from a challenge," Dalton said. "Given the right incentive, I'd imagine the guy's capable of doing just about whatever he sets his mind to."

Wyatt rubbed the back of his neck. "Okay, then, I guess we best get out butts in gear and finish up that roof on the main house. We've got three days before they send Aimee and Grace home."

"Three? These days, they send them home practically overnight if there are no complications." Liberty leaned her arms on the table, capturing Wyatt's gaze.

He held up his hand. "Everything's fine. Gracie's bilirubin, I think they called it, was a little out of whack. They want to keep her for a day or two and *pink her up*, they said. Aimee was a bit anemic, so they're going to keep her in as well so she can go ahead and nurse."

Rein finished his beer. "Good. I'll call Hank and get Clay's contact information and call him myself to make arrangements. I'll say he can move in in a couple of weeks?"

Wyatt nodded. "Yeah, and maybe we can get a concrete path laid out in the meantime."

Dalton nodded, appreciating that the topic had moved forward from the emotional topics of family and the past. He knew how to work hard, play harder—two things he did very well. Handling emotional drama was not his forte. "We've got to get that roof up so my niece can sleep in her room without a bunch of noise." They'd spent the better part of the summer repainting and refurnishing the portion of the house damaged by the fire. Gratefully, End of the Line's finest volunteer firefighters had managed to contain most of the fire to the back of

the house. Still, the completed cabins had come in handy
for the family to have places to stay during the recon-
struction phase.

Ten cabins—some for single occupation, others for
small groups—stretched alongside the creek that flowed
a few hundred yards from the barn. A wide asphalt path
had been planned to provide guests with a short walk
access from the cabins to the main house and everything
in-between.

Dalton stood and tucked his dark hair under his hat.
He owned a Stetson—several, really—but he preferred
the ratty, old Cubs ball cap. Maybe to be different, maybe
because it was all his mother had ever given him. "I'm
going to run down to Tyler's place to make sure he can
come out and take another look at the air conditioner
and electrical wiring before the girls come home."

Wyatt grinned.

"What?" Dalton tossed at his brother.

"Nothing, you just said *the girls*."

Liberty slid out of the booth and kissed Dalton on the
cheek. "You're just an old softie."

Dalton grimaced.

Wyatt cleared his throat. "I'm heading back down to
Billings to give *my girls* a kiss goodnight." He grabbed his
hat. "See you all at home in a bit."

"Guess that leaves you and me, darling. What'll we do
for supper?" Rein asked.

Liberty smiled and pulled him out of the booth. "Take
me home and let's see what we can rustle up."

Rein glanced at Dalton. "I love it when she goes all
cowgirl on me."

"Spare me." Dalton shoved Rein's shoulder, causing
him to stumble as they laughed and followed Liberty out
the door.

∽

A few days had gone by since Angelique had run into Dalton at the hospital, and with work and caring for Emilee, she'd had marginal success in not thinking about how damn good he looked.

Angelique dropped a small bag of groceries in the front seat of her car and looked up in time to see Dalton's impressive Black F-250 roll up to the gas pumps. His gaze behind those dark sunglasses connected to hers for a brief moment and her memory flooded with a play-by-play of the night they'd met in this very store. As she climbed in the car, she reminded herself of what they'd been through, she and Emilee. Delving into her past with the handsome Kinnison who'd once stolen her heart reeked of trouble. What happened between them shouldn't have, plain and simple. Had she been smart, she'd have turned down Sally's invitation to their five-year class reunion in End of the Line. But she'd begged, and Angelique felt the loss of not seeing her friend in years. Passing his truck as she pulled out on the road towards home, she thought back to that night and the events that would change her life forever.

"Can you believe we've been out of school for *five* years?" Sally nudged Angelique who sat next to her at Dusty's. Both of them and another classmate, Evelyn Moore, were nursing special "reunion" margaritas created by Dusty himself. It had been longer than five years since Angelique had moved to Chicago. Last time she saw Sally, they were both too young to step foot in Dusty's bar.

"Omigod. Isn't that Dalton Kinnison playing pool in the back room?" Evelyn whispered, leaning forward.

Sally looked at Angelique with a challenging smile. "I dare you to go say 'hi'."

Angelique tossed her childhood friend a curious look. One reason she'd accepted Sally's invitation was that she'd needed time away from her boyfriend back in Chicago. He'd served two tours of duty and had recently been dishonorably discharged due to a confrontation with a superior. He'd wanted some space, and so had she. The reunion seemed a good excuse. "Probably not a good idea. Besides, he doesn't remember me."

Sally's arm shot up as she waved across the room to get his attention. "Too late, he's coming over. Holy cow, the man keeps looking better and better."

Angelique watched Sally's face, knowing by the joyous look in her eyes that he was standing right behind her. "Hey, Dalton. How's that good-looking brother of yours?"

"Sitting home pining away that he's not out with you tonight, I suspect."

His voice, precisely as she remembered, reverberated in Angelique's heart. The crush she'd had on him was maddening, insane if you look at the fact that he was an upperclassman and didn't know she was alive. Wait, what did he say? "You're dating a Kinnison?" She looked at Sally, aghast at the revelation.

"Just started dating Rein. Did I forget to mention that?" She shrugged.

"So, Evelyn, how's it going?" A shadow fell over the table as Dalton moved around so that Angelique had to face him without being rude. She made a mental note to drop Sally head first off the nearest cliff. He slid into the booth next to Evelyn, who nearly fainted. Angelique rolled her eyes, tossed aside the straw, and drank deeply of her margarita.

"Well, this is a fine group of lovely ladies." His gaze swung to hers. "I don't believe we've met. I'm Dalton Kinnison."

Angelique stared at him, hoping he'd remember her name. The knowledge that he didn't was superseded by her preoccupation of how damn fine he looked. He'd not only matured well, but working hard and outdoor living made him even more handsome.

A shadow of a beard framed his solid jaw and his hair was longer than she remembered in high school. He wore it just above his collar, tucked behind his ears. And lord have mercy, when he smiled those eyes the color of fine whiskey glittered with life. She pulled herself from his mesmerizing gaze and looked to Sally, pleading silently for help. She felt the heat rising to her face. "Sorry, I 've got to go." Angelique scooted out of the booth and headed for the door. "I'll talk to you tomorrow."

"Good to see you, Angelique. Don't stay away so long next time," Dusty called out to her with a wave of his bar towel. She glanced over her shoulder in time to see Dalton's startled face. She just prayed that Sally wouldn't share with him the massive crush she used to have on him before she was forced to move to Chicago with her mom.

She hurried to her old car, grateful that it had started and was almost to the road toward the house when she realized her aunt had asked her to stop at the store. With an exasperated sigh that Dalton Kinnison could still rattle her cage, she pulled the car around and into the Git-n-Go parking lot. There was a chill in the air and it smelled like rain. Stepping from the car, she glanced up to see thick black storm clouds rolling in over the mountains. Hurrying inside she found the refrigerated section at the back of the store and stood searching for the brand of butter her aunt had requested.

The bell on the door gave notice of another customer.

"Hey, Travis, how's it going?"

She glanced down the aisle in time to see Dalton step up to peruse the cold beer in the cooler. Seeing him, she allowed a quick skim of his fine, muscular body honed from hard work, no doubt on the ranch. He was dressed casually in faded jeans and an untucked snap rodeo shirt, and her heartbeat kicked up a notch imagining the body underneath it all. She chose to blame Dusty and his special "reunion" margarita for the confused way she felt. Blinking from her daze, she grabbed the butter and ducked behind a display of bagged snacks, hoping he hadn't seen her.

"Are you avoiding me, Angelique?"

Damn. Her heart came to an abrupt stop as she looked up and met his wicked grin. *Stay calm. Just speak to the man. How hard can it be?* "Of course not. It was clear you didn't remember me, which is nothing new, honestly." She waved her hand, dismissing the situation, him, and her wayward emotions. "Listen, really, it's okay. See ya." She turned on her heel.

"Hey."

Do not turn around. "Yeah?" She spun to face him and slapped on a smile. *Be brave, girl.*

He frowned and shifted his six-pack to the other hand. "I'm sorry I didn't recognize you. I guess we all change over the years."

Yes, and you look even hotter. She sighed, uncertain it was wise to dredge up emotions, dangerous emotions that she had over time and with great care tucked neatly away in her brain.

"You definitely have." He smiled.

"For the better, I hope?"

His smile widened. "Hell, yeah, girl."

Okay, then, now what? Angelique searched for something to say to the man who had dominated most of her teenage dreams.

"Where are you now?"

She blinked, realizing she'd been mesmerized yet again by his captivating eyes. "Um...still in Chicago."

"Yeah, you and your mom moved there before my sophomore year, I think, wasn't it?"

He remembered this how? "Um, yeah, she met a guy, and for a while it looked like it would work, but it didn't. And mom started drinking again, so much so that she wrapped her car around a telephone pole one night." She stopped suddenly and realized how callous she sounded. "I'm sorry. I guess I'm a little desensitized."

"Sorry, that must have been pretty rough."

She chuckled quietly. "You have no idea."

He studied her for a moment and she knew he didn't have more to say. Truly, what more did they have in common?

"Listen, it was great to see you. Take care." She quickly paid for her items and was grateful for the cool, fine mist that had started. Sticking her keys in the ignition, she turned it. Getting no sound, she tried twice more but with the same results and a check engine light. Pounding her hand against the wheel, she started to call Sally, but a tap on the window startled her. She rolled it down.

"Trouble?"

She swallowed, staring into the eyes of what surely was trouble and always had been. "Won't start. Engine light comes on."

The mist had turned to a steady rain. "Listen, I'll drop you at home. No one is going to get out tonight in this."

What choice did she have? "If you're sure you don't mind?" She gathered her things, and he grabbed her hand as the gentle rain turned to a frog-strangling downpour.

Tucked inside the cab of his truck was the epitome of her teenage angst. How many times had she wished for this? She laughed, not realizing she'd done so out loud.

"What is it?"

"Nothing."

"Come on," he said, poking her arm. "What are you

thinking?"

She brushed back the now-sodden strands of hair from her face. "Tell me what you're up to these days, Dalton."

He shrugged as the truck came to life, its gigantic motor sounding as though it could eat her car for breakfast. "Working at the ranch. Rein and I handle the cattle sales; Wyatt pretty much stays on property handling things there."

"I'm sorry about Jed. I didn't hear about it until later. I feel like I've been gone forever."

"It's okay. Jed made sure we knew how to run every aspect of the ranch. We're keeping things going, hanging in there, you know." He pulled the truck out of the space and hesitated before turning toward her aunt and uncle's place. "Hey, have you seen the new addition to the school? They put in a skywalk between the middle and high schools."

She chuckled, remembering how many times she'd trudged through the snow to a class held in the other building. "That would've been handy on the number of tennis shoes I ruined in the snow."

He laughed, and though he didn't ask if she wanted to, he turned toward the school. "It's pretty impressive, really, especially for a school that size. And they've put up a new football field with metal bleachers. I hear rumblings of a new baseball diamond next year." He waggled his brows and turned to her with a big grin. "Next thing you know they'll be putting in those new-fangled automated hand-dryers in the restrooms," he said with a laugh.

She laughed with him, and while her heart cautioned her to be wary, she enjoyed this more open, friendlier version of Dalton.

He followed the road to the edge of town and turned into the parking lot of the school. Finding a spot where the headlights illuminated the new field and the annex, he shut off his truck. They sat in silence staring at the structure. Angelique's mind raced with a million scenarios, most of them involving her avid crush on Dalton. "Plan to drink all those yourself?"

He glanced at her in mild surprise, unbuckled, then reached over the seat, grabbed two beers, and handed her one. She unbuckled, accepted the bottle and took one long swallow. "Thanks."

He took a pull on his and leaned back in his seat. "I used to love hanging out here after school. Football and baseball practice every night. Guess that sounds pretty pathetic, pining over your glory days, doesn't it?"

She shrugged, wishing she'd had the chance to participate more instead of caring for her mom. "You were good. I always thought you'd go further with your baseball career."

"Really?" He brushed his dark hair back over his head, revealing his chiseled features.

"Why didn't you? You went to college, right?"

He stared into the semi-darkness. Only four tall light poles illuminated the deserted parking lot. They flickered and a flash of lightening split across the black sky. The lights went out, plunging them into blackness.

He picked up the conversation as though nothing had happened. "I don't know, I guess after Jed died I felt I needed to be there for Wyatt and Rein."

Angelique nodded and finished her beer, her brain settling into the sweet buzz of the number of drinks she'd had. "I understand."

He leaned forward and put his hands on the keys. "Yeah, I don't think so."

"Trust me, Dalton," she said, placing her hand over his." I know what it's like to have to put your dreams on hold."

"It sucks," he responded quietly, not looking at her, not moving away from her touch.

She was playing a dangerous game. God help her, she was on fire. Every fantasy, every dream was roiling inside her, fueled by the storm raging outside. A gust of wind rocked the truck and his eyes met hers.

"I should get you home," he said.

Angelique held his gaze and nodded. Then his mouth was on hers, his hands pushing aside the buttons of her blouse. Frantic, needing to touch his skin, she tugged his t-shirt over his head, pressing her palms against his rockhard chest.

His hands skimmed over her flesh, leaving her shaking with need. His hungry mouth found hers, drugging her senses, exceeding her every fantasy. In a tangle of limbs, ferocious need stripped away all barriers between them. Easing the seat to allow more room, he cradled the small of her back, teasing her with teeth and tongue until she squirmed against his hardening length. She met his heated gaze as he moved his hand down her belly, stroking the ache between her thighs, igniting her body and bringing her to a dizzying height until she surrendered with an audible sigh. "I want you," she whispered against his lips as she lifted to accept him, joining her body—long awaited—to his.

Rain pounded against the windows, coming down in heavy sheets that blew across the lot. Steam fogged the windows as she rode him, clinging to his waist, feeling his hard muscles bunch and move beneath her palms. Furious, unrelenting, they drove each other, building, pushing until her body splintered apart. She clung to his firm shoulders, riding his fervent, deep thrusts, climaxing again as he followed her over.

The sound of the wind and rain echoed across the roof, permeating the silence.

She lay across him, his heart pounding wildly against hers. After a moment, she felt his hands slide up her arms, easing her upright.

"Wow." His sexy grin followed, but little else. She should've known better not to dream of promises, or confessions of unrequited love. In an instant, she saw the guarded curtain fall over his face.

"Yeah, wow," she repeated. Clearly, neither had meant for this to happen.

Amid hooded glances, neither spoke as they hastily dressed. She moved back to the passenger seat and wrapped the seat belt over her still thrumming body. Dalton sat for a moment with his hands on the wheel, staring out the window.

"Your aunt and uncle will be wondering where you are."

Angelique fought to stay composed. She'd made the first move, given him the green light and hadn't stopped when things got heated.

Like a couple of reckless school kids.

"Probably," she answered.

He started the truck and didn't speak again until he'd pulled into the gravel drive of her aunt and uncle's house. He kept the motor idling, offering no acknowledgment of what had just occurred between them.

Confused, she chided herself for her behavior and quickly unbuckled. Gathering her things, she paused. "It was good to see you, Dalton."

His dark eyes met hers and his closed expression spoke volumes about the enormous mistake she'd made. Had she really thought she could win over Dalton Kinnison with her sexual prowess? She lifted her chin, determined to hang on to her pride. Well, she'd gotten *that* fantasy out of her system. It was time to move on. "Good luck with the ranch."

"Yeah, good luck to you, too. Good to see you."

He swallowed hard, the corner of his mouth lifted in an attempted smile before he averted his eyes from hers. "Oh, Angelique?" He reached over the back of the seat. "You almost forgot this."

She took the grocery bag and, mentally smacking herself, climbed from the truck. Closing the door gently, she glanced at the dark house, relieved that no one seemed awake. She needed to think things through. *Maybe he just needs some time to process what happened? Or maybe you're living on a cloud, Angelique, and its time you got your feet on the ground.* The roar of his truck made her wince as he drove off. She tiptoed up the front porch steps.

"You've been with Dalton Kinnison?" a voice issued from the front porch swing. It was her Aunt Rebecca, still awake and waiting, it appeared, for her.

"We met at the grocery store, drove around a bit and talked. That's all." Angelique stood poised at the front door. She was no longer a child, but that did not quell the sense that she'd just acted like an idiot schoolgirl.

"Surprised he spoke to you. We haven't had contact with any of the Kinnisons since Wyatt let go the majority of the crew Jed had out there for years. It was difficult for your uncle, being Jed's right hand man and closest friend."

She hesitated, her hand on the doorknob. "Don't worry, Aunt Rebecca. I won't be seeing him again." She faced her then, plastering an overly bright smile on her face. "Besides, I have a great guy waiting for me back in Chicago, remember?"

A long stretch of silence followed.

"You've not spoken much about your mother since you've been here."

"You mean *your* sister?" Bitterness scalded her tongue.

"She was your mother Angelique."

"She was a worthless, strung-out piece of crap," she blurted out in anger.

Her aunt leaped from the chair and in two strides stood nose-to-nose with her.

Angelique held her ground. "You can't possibly think to defend her, not now, not after everything," Angelique snapped. Hurt. Angry. Reeling still from Dalton's dismissal. Why should she care? Was he any better than the man who waited for her back home? *Home. Hell, where was that?*

Rebecca's gaze softened. Her hands framed Angelique's face as she spoke. "We don't get to pick the family we're born to." Her voice lowered, soft and soothing. "But we all have choices—some good, some bad. You can think everyone is out to make a fool of you and everyone else is to blame. Eventually, you're the one who ends up fooling yourself. Learn from her mistakes, Angelique, but do not become embittered by them."

Angelique stared at her aunt's kind brown eyes shimmering in the pale yard light. How many times had she been left there when her mother would have leave on business trips, some of them more than a week? Angelique grew up doing chores on the farm, learning to cook at her aunt's side. They'd given her a life. Perspective has a funny way of providing clarity. "I know, Aunt Rebecca. I hear you." She drew the woman close, grateful for the closeness, for all she'd taught her. And realized suddenly how her aunt seemed smaller and more frail than she remembered.

Chapter Three

"WHAT DO YOU THINK?" REIN waited to get feedback from the rest of the group gathered around the Kinnison dinner table. It had been built by Rein to accommodate their family meals, its dual purpose now served family meetings.

Dalton downed his second cup of coffee, needing the caffeine after a number of sleepless nights. Each time he ran into Angelique, it became harder to put behind him the memories he'd fought long and hard to forget. He stared at the flat screen television hung on one wall of the dining room. Wired up to a new security system, the television by decree of Aimee, would not be on during meals, but was useful at other times in providing surveillance of several areas of the house and property. Wyatt insisted on installing the system after the arson incident, sighting that it would be beneficial as added security for cabin tenants as well.

The video they'd just previewed showed an advertisement created by Liberty to showcase the Last Hope ranch, its mission, and amenities, including trail rides, nature hikes, and fishing. Liberty retrieved the DVD and scanned the faces at the table. "Well?"

Rein glanced at his business partner and new wife, smiling at her with a wink.

Aimee placed baby Grace over her shoulder and gently rocked her side to side. "I think it's beautiful. What are your plans for it?"

Liberty's eyes lit up. "First, we connect with the cham-

ber in town, get them on board with our project. Then
maybe make copies of this DVD and send it out to various hospitals and tourism sites along with our brochure.
We could build up to magazines, online advertising, radio, and who knows, maybe television spots?"

"The idea," Rein interjected, "is to get the word out
about the ranch. We've gotten all the formal paperwork
in place, so now we can focus on our mission for the
ranch. How to make it what Jed envisioned."

"A place for second chances." Wyatt tapped his finger
on the table.

"A place for people to heal both physically and emo-
tionally," Rein added.

"If I may address the topic of physical healing?" Michael Greyfeather spoke in his calm, quiet way.

Rein nodded. "Absolutely."

"My purpose here is to care for the overflow of re-
covered horses from the Mountain Sunrise Ranch. And
they are indeed grateful for your generosity in allowing
the horses to be cared for here until forever families can
adopt them. However, since learning that the first guest
of the Last Hope Ranch is a wounded war veteran, I feel
I may be able to offer something more."

"Go on." Rein sat forward, listening intently.

"As it happens, I am a certified equine therapist and
before coming back to the ranch to assist here, I was on
a team at Mountain Sunrise that offers a similar program
to what I think you may be discussing here."

Puzzled, Dalton looked at Michael, his brown skin
leathered from years in the sun. "When did you have
time to get certified?"

Michael smiled and glanced at Wyatt. "It is no secret
that I have dedicated my life to working with horses.
I trained the first horses Jed ever gave you boys and I
continued to break horses and care for neglected horses

long before it became a popular accreditation. After your uncle passed and the ranch crew downsized, I decided to check into training. Much of that training was no more than an affirmation of all that'd I'd been taught growing up on the reservation. But it helped me to network with people who used horse therapy as a tool for healing. What I have come to know is that the broken spirit of a horse is not far different from the spirit of a person. Horses can feel more than you realize and can be highly effective in the healing process."

Rein straightened in his chair. "This is amazing. It's exactly what we need." He turned to Wyatt. "I propose that we make Michael head of our equine therapy. Dalton"—he looked at his brother—"you could help him, and maybe get trained yourself."

Dalton had followed the conversation, and while he agreed that it sounded like something that Jed would have wanted, he wasn't sure if it was a good fit for him. There'd been days lately when he felt more of a candidate for the Last Hope Ranch than one of its co-owners.

"If this is a direction you'd like to pursue, I can check with the owner of Sunrise and see if they'd be willing to come down and look at our facility. Perhaps they could lend us a horse trained to handle our special guests."

Wyatt broke his silence, his gaze staying on Michael. "I owe you an apology, Michael, one that's long overdue. When Jed died, I let everyone go. I nearly lost the ranch. It wasn't a good time and it was poor judgment on my part."

"Wyatt," Michael responded with quiet diligence. "Had circumstances not been what they were, I might never have had the incentive to follow through. To be honest, it was Rebecca's idea. I think she tired of me being underfoot." Kindness showed in his easy smile. "Nothing is ever wasted if something good can come of it. Jed would understand. And now we have come full circle and are in a better place to help build a future and do some good."

Wyatt rose and pulled the old man into a bear hug. The two men patted each other on the back.

"I have asked Angelique to stop down later today to look at a one of the horses. She has been at my side and has worked with a variety of equine since she was old enough to ride. Perhaps she, too, would have time to volunteer on weekends."

"Oh, then you have to ask Sally, too." Aimee piped up. "She'd love that. Especially if it involved trail rides for kids. She's about the most patient person I know." Grace squawked, signaling the need for a diaper change. "If you'll excuse me." She smiled and rose from the table, unable to leave until Wyatt kissed his daughter's rose-petal cheek.

"Let me help you." Liberty skirted around the table with a gleeful smile as she followed Aimee.

"Oh, honey, be sure to remind everyone about what we need for the BBQ next Saturday, and be sure to show them plans for the new fire pit." Aimee puckered her lips and gave Wyatt a wink.

"New fire pit?" Rein turned his focus on Wyatt.

"Later." Wyatt looked at Dalton. "You haven't said a whole lot. What do you think?"

Dalton was sure he could handle the horse end of things, the repairs, and the daily upkeep of the cabins and property. Hell, maybe even the training if it came to that, but having Angelique here underfoot on weekends? *That,* he *wasn't* sure about. "Excuse me, I need a refill."

He pushed from the table and escaped to the kitchen. Filling his cup, he pondered the wisdom of topping it with a touch of whiskey. He took in the view of pristine summer sky framing the mountains and thought back to high school and the girl he'd seen that day on his way home.

He'd just gotten his driver's license and had been at baseball practice in town. He'd hung around a little too long showing off the old, beat-up truck the three boys shared and realized it was getting late to do his chores before supper. Jed was strict that chores came before anyone ate. Fortunately, there was an old gravel road just past Dusty's Bar that provided a shortcut home. As he came around the bend, probably driving too fast, he spotted a figure hunched forward on a dark-colored horse. The rider, bent forward, rode as though being chased by a demon. He recognized the long, dark braid belonging to Angelique, Michael Greyfeather's shy young niece, who he thought was maybe a grade or two behind him in school, though he hadn't ever paid much attention…until now. Fascinated, he slowed the truck, nearly driving off into the ditch as he watched her handle the horse— confident, determined, and fearless. Something stirred in his gut. She wasn't his type, yet she stayed in his thoughts long after he'd gotten home that night, leaving him totally puzzled. Much as she'd done since coming back to End of the Line.

"Are you having second thoughts about the plans for the ranch?"

Pulled back to the present, Dalton shrugged and turned to face Rein standing at the kitchen door. "Nope. Jed started this place as a cattle ranch, ran it like that for years. The fact that he wrote down his thoughts for renaming it the Last Hope Ranch makes me think that he knew the cattle industry was struggling—at least in the way he'd always known it to be." Dalton looked down at his cup, no longer desiring the coffee. "He did it because of us—you, me, and Wyatt. He took the three of us"—Dalton looked out the window and took a steadying breath before continuing—"and saw something in how he and this ranch changed us, made us better, gave us purpose. He thought exposure here for other folks would produce the same results. I get that. I'm grateful for it."

Rein walked in, leaned against the counter, and folded his arms over his chest. "So, what is it, then?"

"Hey, what are you two plotting now?" Wyatt reached into the refrigerator and pulled out a tub of fresh blueberries. He nudged Rein aside, grabbed a bowl, and filled it.

Rein released a quiet sigh. "Just trying to see what's wrong with little Lucy over here." He tipped his head toward Dalton.

Wyatt's gaze darted to Dalton. "Tell me you aren't involved with that pool shark blonde from Billings again. That woman stalked you for weeks."

Dalton frowned. "Damn, would you two give me a break?"

A berry *pinged* him on the forehead and he swatted at it, throwing Wyatt a stern look. "Don't start with me, Wyatt." Another berry whizzed past him. "All right, that does it." Dalton searched for the first thing he could lay his hands on. A tea towel hanging on a hook was the best he could do. He tried rolling it in his hands, ready to snap his brother. Rein stood off to the side, doubled over in laughter.

Aimee appeared at the kitchen door, baby Grace cradled in her arms. "Wyatt Kinnison, where are my—are you throwing *my* blueberries at your brother?"

"Busted," Dalton said with a grin and returned the towel to its place.

Aimee stuck her hand out and, with a chagrined look, Wyatt handed her the bowl. Eyeing the three of them, she turned on her heel and walked out.

"She's been eating blueberries by the ton," Dalton commented after she left.

Wyatt shrugged and popped a last berry in his mouth. "Nuts, water, oatmeal, snow peas, eggs…she claims it's supposed to increase lactation."

"As in nursing, you mean?" Dalton baited his brother with a wicked grin.

"You don't want to go there," Wyatt warned.

"Hey, paybacks are hell." He grinned. "So, does this mean you know that you're off limits until she finishes nursing?"

Wyatt straightened his gaze firm on his brother. "Are you seriously asking this?"

Dalton shrugged. Honestly, he found it a viable question. One he might tuck away for future reference.

"And you think my photos of childbirth are sick?"

"Hey, it's an honest question," Rein interjected on Dalton's behalf.

Dalton nodded his appreciation toward Rein.

"Shut up." Wyatt turned to Rein. "Besides, I'm pretty sure the conversation you two were having wasn't about my wife's breasts."

"Honey?" Aimee stood again in the doorway, curiosity etched on her face. "What's going on?"

Wyatt narrowed his gaze on Dalton as he placed his arm around his wife's shoulder. "Just my idiot brothers, sweetheart. Pay no attention to them."

"Hey, don't call me an idiot," Rein called after the departing pair. His gaze swung back to Dalton. "Clever, by the way, how you managed to side-step answering my question."

Dalton blew out a sigh. "Did you ever feel like you weren't sure if you belonged somewhere?"

"Sit," Rein ordered pointing to a kitchen chair. "Tell me what's going on in that head of yours."

Reluctantly, he slid in the chair and folded his hands on the table.

"Go on. I'm listening."

Dalton stared for a moment at his hands uncertain he could put into words how he felt without sounding like a whiny-ass baby. Hearts-to-heart were not his thing. He'd just as soon take his fishing pole, head up to the cabin in the woods that Jed had built for hunting and sort things out on his own. But this was different. He didn't know how to shake these feelings roiling around inside him. He didn't know how to shake his memories of *her.*

"So, is it the plans for the ranch not suiting you, or something else?"

He and Rein, closer in age, had gone off to college together while Wyatt stayed back and ran the ranch— nearly into the ground, but that wasn't the point just now. The pair had gone on after graduation to handle the cattle sales, spending long hours looking over contracts, negotiating the best prices to restaurants and the like for their cattle. But when it came to personal issues, Rein nearly had to pry it out of Dalton.

He glanced at Rein. Though he was the older sibling, it seemed Dalton found himself coming to his younger brother for advice. "It's not the ranch, the horses, or the cabins," Dalton stated.

"Well, then it must be a woman." Rein knocked his fist on the table. "And since I know it's not Sally, I'm guessing it's Angelique."

"You're nuts." Dalton wondered if he was that transparent.

"Listen, I know something happened between you two."

"What are you talking about?" Dalton hadn't breathed a word to anyone about the night he and Angelique had shared. "Who told you, Sally?"

"Look," Rein held up his hand. "Before you go all Clint Eastwood on Sally's ass, she doesn't know details. But let's face it, it's been no secret that since the wedding you've been avoiding the woman like the plague." He studied Dalton. "Something you'd like to talk about in that department?"

Dalton held his brother's gaze. "No."

Rein eyed him a moment more, sighed, and looked away. "Fine. So, you're good with her working around here a bit more?"

Dalton scratched at a nick on the Formica tabletop. "Sure." He heard Rein snort.

"You're lying through your teeth and this may be something you want to work out alone, I get that. But what I am more concerned about is this 'unsure if you belong here' shit."

"I didn't say here, I said somewhere."

"Right. So, explain it to me, because I'm about ready to bust a chair over your head if you don't."

He shoved away from the table and stalked to the back door, stuffing his hands in his pockets. He remembered barbecues, times when the three would sit out on the deck after supper and look at the stars; the times Jed let them go up to the hunting cabin to sleep over. As oldest, the ranch belonged to Wyatt, though they shared in its upkeep. The cabins had become Rein's project, though Dalton had helped build them, but he realized lately that he'd spent most of his life since college looking for a good time. He hadn't given much thought to the fact that one day it might catch up to him. Hell, the other day in the mirror he'd seen traces of silver woven into his dark hair. "What have I done with my life?" Frustration laced with his words.

"What?"

He glanced over his shoulder. "You heard me. You and

Wyatt. You have the ranch and the cabins, you both have wives and families—well, prospects, anyway." He raked his hand through his hair, suddenly feeling years older.

"You're serious?" Rein asked.

"Hey, you wanted to know."

"I had no idea that you felt something was missing from your life. Figured you were happy being unattached."

"I am." Dalton frowned. "I was…I am. Hell if I know. Just not feeling myself lately, I guess."

Rein nodded. "I get that." He eyed Dalton before he spoke, "You know, after my folks died and I came to live here, I remember feeling that way."

Dalton looked at him in disbelief. "Jed was your uncle. You're the one who should have felt you belonged here. We were the vagrants."

Rein shook his head. "Nope. You can say what you want, but by the time I got here, Jed had already taught you both everything about the ranch. He'd adopted you by choice. I was the vagrant."

"Come on, man." Dalton began to realize how perspective could change everything.

"Hey, it's the truth. I don't feel that way anymore, but it's not because of the cabins or that Jed was my uncle. It's because I belong to a family. Brothers I could count on, watch my back, kick me in the ass when I need it, get into trouble with." Rein grinned. "You belong here, with your family. All Jed's dreams, all the work to make this ranch viable again doesn't mean jack shit without you here to help see it through."

Pressure built in Dalton's chest. He swallowed a lump in his throat and shook his head. Feeling Rein's hand on his shoulder, he looked into his brother's concerned gaze.

"Look, I don't know what's going on between you and Angelique. But whatever it is, wouldn't it be better to stay and face it down like every other challenge you've ever encountered?"

He considered Rein's words. Maybe his brother had a point. Maybe it was better to resolve this tension—whatever it was—between him and Angelique. He slapped Rein on the arm. "I don't know, but thanks for listening to my bull."

Rein nodded and pulled Dalton into a man hug.

"As adorable as this is, you guys think you might get your asses in gear?" Wyatt stood, arms folded, leaning against the doorframe. "The paver and asphalt guys are here. That pathway isn't going to build itself."

As Dalton walked with Rein down the porch steps, he felt a nudge on his arm.

"Hey, you know if you ever want to pursue this idea of finding your birth father, Liberty is damn good on the computer."

Dalton tossed his brother a half-smile. "One challenge at a time, bro. One challenge at a time."

∞

Angelique picked at her salad, trying valiantly to ignore Sally's remarks. "I'm so glad you called. It feels like I've hardly seen you since the wedding. How's the job… and other things?"

Angelique glanced at Sally, aware of where her friend was headed. "And, no, I'm not seeing anyone. The clinic keeps me pretty busy and then I want to be home with Emilee."

"Did I say anything about dating?" Sally looked surprised, but her smile showed her true implication. "Besides, I think it's wonderful that you and Emilee spend time together." She shrugged. "I love my kids at school, but now and again it'd be nice to have someone who'd, you know, care for me."

"What are you getting at, Ms. Andersen?"

"Me? Nothing."

"Right. As if you don't think I didn't notice how you gushed all over Aimee and Wyatt at the wedding. And don't tell me that you didn't have something to do with Rein and Liberty finally seeing eye to eye."

Sally shrugged. "Just a nudge here and there. Then I just let nature take its course."

"And what about you? I thought I saw you talking with Rein's friend Hank after they got home from Vegas." Angelique crooked her brow.

"Hank is a very nice guy. I've known him a long time. His sister, ugh, what a nightmare."

"And Hank?" Angelique prodded. It felt good to chat about everyday mundane things, rediscovering normal life like reading to her daughter, baking with her aunt, girl talk with Sally.

She lifted a shoulder. "I don't know. He's okay, I suppose. Not really my type."

Angelique smiled and popped a cucumber slice in her mouth. She couldn't fault her friend for being selective when it came to men. God knows she should've made better choices. But the past was in the rearview mirror, at least for the moment. She'd chosen to keep that part of her life private and for all anyone in End of the Line knew, her husband had died a hero in the Middle East conflict. As long as he was in prison and adhered to the no contact decree of the divorce, to her, he was dead.

"There's always Tyler." Sally smiled.

Sally was on a roll. "The plumber from Tyler Plumbing and Heating? Oh, wait, I remember him from the wedding. Turned out okay. He was that geeky kid in my seventh-grade science class." Her smile faded as the reality of her childhood invaded her memory. Her life back then had been gobbled up with caring for her alcoholic mother, hiding the truth from the rest of the town.

She had few memories of friends, dances, the stuff that most kids did. Football games were her singular indulgence. She attended every home game and for one reason alone—to watch Dalton Kinnsion play.

Even then, she should have known that eventually he'd break her heart, but she was a starry-eyed freshman, smitten with the upperclassmen bad boy. Lord, how she'd admired his fearless swagger, how he crossed the line—whether coming to class late or ducking into the boy's room for a quick smoke. He barely acknowledged her presence, but in her eyes, he was the epitome of freedom—dark, forbidden, reckless. She was head over heels in love.

"There's plenty of time yet to get back into the dating pool. Billings is full of cute guys. It's around here in End of the Line that the *pickins'* are a tad slim."

"Just a tad?" Angelique chuckled.

"Well, isn't this wonderful to see you two out for a girls' lunch." Betty, owner and head cook of the newly renovated Betty's café, refilled each of their water glasses. The lunch crowd had long since dissipated, which had been Angelique's hope in avoiding those curious to know why she'd come back to End of the Line.

"It's great to see you back in town, Angelique—or do you prefer Angie?" Betty smiled, but Angelique could see the curiosity in Betty's eyes.

"Either is fine. I do love what you've done with the place, Betty."

The older woman's face beamed with pride as she glanced around the room. "I have Miss Liberty Belle Mackenzie to thank for that. She came in and, with that creative magic of hers, transformed this entire place. We've even gotten a four-star rating from the *Billings Gazette*, best little dining experience in southwest Montana, they said."

"Congratulations," Angelique said. "That's big news around here."

Betty laughed. "Honey, any news is big news around here. Speaking of news, are you two planning to go to the Kinnison BBQ next Saturday? Wyatt and Aimee want to thank everyone who helped get the house restored and the cabins up and running." Betty grinned. "If you ask me, that Wyatt just wants to show off his gorgeous wife and baby girl."

"As well he should," Sally stated. "Both are gorgeous. Those boys have worked hard to create the legacy that Jed left behind. I wouldn't miss it for the world. In fact, I was just about to ask Angelique to be my date." She tossed her a smile.

Angelique opened her mouth to graciously decline, but Betty, oblivious, forged ahead, her eyes welling. "Those boys sure have come a long way, that's true. Poor dears. I remember the first time Jed brought them in here. They were in a world of hurt, those three. And now, well…" She sniffed and waved away her emotions. "They've all turned out to be men Jed would be proud to call his sons."

Sally sighed. "Yep, and just think, only one eligible Kinnsion male left." Sally waggled her brows.

Angelique narrowed her gaze at her friend.

"Merciful heavens. I didn't mean to go on so and interrupt your girl time. By the way, we've got some of your aunt's double Dutch apple pie left if you all want a slice for dessert." She winked and walked away, humming a carefree tune as she straightened chairs.

Sally picked up her glass, settled back in her chair, and eyed Angelique.

"What?"

"I just wondered if you remembered all those apple pies you used to leave in a certain upperclassman's beat up old truck."

The moment Betty mentioned the sweet treat, Angelique's memory of sneaking them on the front seat kicked in. Not that it mattered now, but to admit her remembering it to Sally was akin to setting wild horses free.

"I think you must have me mixed up with someone else."

"Oh, no. I also remember that you let that bitch Bonnie Stillman take credit for them."

"Bonnie Stillman. Where'd she wind up?" Angelique did her best to sidetrack Sally.

"Waitressing at Dusty's Bar for a while. I heard she moved to California last year to try to get into television."

Though there was no reason why that news should make her happy, it did. "Good for her. I seem to remember Dalton dating just about every female in school, didn't he?"

Sally chuckled and offered a nod.

Angelique smiled and gave her friend a quizzical look.

Sally's hand shot up in defense. "Oh, hell, no. My mother would've skinned me alive if I'd gotten within ten feet of that boy." She shook her head. "He definitely had a rep, didn't he?"

Angelique picked at her salad, looking for a way to change the topic. "Indeed, and it doesn't appear that he's changed much. I've heard he spends a lot of time at Dusty's. Aunt Rebecca mentioned something about a fight with a few locals a while back—New Year's Eve, I think she said?"

Sally lifted a shoulder. "Yeah, pretty exciting night for End of the Line. We were having a fundraiser and this guy came on to Aimee—unsolicited, I might add. Wyatt and Aimee left rather abruptly and the guy—stupid as hell if you ask me—and his friends ganged up on Wyatt. Naturally, the Kinnison boys stick together." Sally continued. "As any good brothers would do, I suspect. Anyway, Wyatt *kind of* came unglued on the guy and then Aimee came unglued on Wyatt. I didn't see her or him the rest of the night, but guessing it must have been a turning point in their relationship, because next thing you know, we're planning a wedding at the ranch."

Angelique laughed. "Dalton always did love a good fight. He had enough detention to show for it."

"Well, he's very protective of his own, that much I know. It sounds like maybe you've been thinking a lot more about Dalton than you care to admit."

Angelique stopped her with an upturned hand. "I admit I might have been a little interested at first. But he's made it pretty clear he wants to keep things distant."

Sally studied her. "Look, I don't know everything. Someday I hope you'll feel like talking about it, but I know you've been though a lot. I know your marriage wasn't ideal. But time changes people, my friend. Dalton has some issues, but what man doesn't? All in all, though, he's a good man."

Angelique sighed, remembering the conversation she and her daughter had had in the car the other day. "I'm sure you're right." She held her hand up to gain Betty's attention and glanced at her friend. "Listen, I'm not interested in dating anyone just yet. Thanks, Betty." She smiled accepting the ticket from the older woman.

"My treat next time." Sally pointed a finger at Angelique. "Regarding Mr. Dalton, who, in case you hadn't noticed, is impossibly gorgeous—just sayin'. You're bound to run into him now and again with your entire family working out at the ranch these days."

"And I'll handle it, thank you. This reminds me, my uncle asked me to run by and take a look at one of the horses. I need to pick up Emilee anyway. Aunt Rebecca insisted on staying to fix supper. Uncle Mike mentioned

they've been working hard to get a pathway built con-
necting the cabins to the main house."

"Yep, I guess they have their first guest arriving soon.
Hey, Rein asked me to stop by sometime and check the
cabin designed for physically challenged guests. Now's as
good a time as any—would you mind if I rode out there
with you? I'll leave my car here, and you can drop me
back off at my car afterwards, if you don't mind."

"My uncle mentioned the new guest. An old college
buddy, I heard."

"Yep, his name is Clay Saunders. Clay, Hank, Dalton,
and Rein were friends at college, is my understanding."
Sally hefted her large purse over her shoulder and followed Angelique outside. "He's a wounded warrior, I
guess. Middle East conflict. Sounds like he's had a rough
time since he got back."

"It's nice that they're still watching out for each other.
And it's nice that you and Rein stayed friends even after
you stopped dating and that he values your opinion."

"He helped me a lot when we ended up having to
remodel dad's house when his Multiple Sclerosis got
worse."

Angelique looked over the hood of her car at Sally.
"I'm so sorry I wasn't there for you back then."

They climbed in the car. "I know you would have
been if you hadn't had a lot on your plate at the time."
She shrugged and looked out the window. "There were
days that it was hard, but dad always tried to make me
feel better, you know? The difficult times made me realize I'm a lot stronger than I thought. And I became a
student of just about every aspect of creating handicap
accessibility in a single-house dwelling."

Angelique grabbed Sally's hand and squeezed it. "I
hope you know how lucky you are to have had the parents you had. And I don't say that to solicit any pity on

me. I really mean it. I'm glad for you."

Her friend studied her. "You had to take care of your mom and were still underage when you moved away. You could have left when things got rough, after your mom passed. But you didn't. I'm sure there are folks who pity me at almost thirty-two and never been married, because I had to take care of my dad and never really had the time or energy to date."

"Well, you're not exactly a spinster, Miss Sally." Angelique smiled as she started her car. There was so much Sally still didn't know about her life in Chicago. One day, maybe, she'd be ready to share it. Just now, though, she wanted to keep moving forward and leave her past in the past.

Sally buckled her seat belt. "True, but I have to be content with how things go, either way. I can't imagine leaving End of the Line. I love my students, the school, when people say hi to each other on the street. I'm just a small-town girl, I guess."

"I'm grateful that Emilee has had the chance to grow up here, but it's been hard these days to drag her away from the ranch."

"Is she getting attached to Gracie?"

They sped along the mountain pass road on the way to the Kinnison's ranch. "She's become quite the little mother, but she's also excited to help my uncle with the horses. She wants to be in the middle of everything."

"She's a good kid." Sally patted her arm. "I can't believe how mature she was during that accident last winter with the school suburban. I remember that she told Aimee that she could be a brave hero, like her father."

Angelique's face flushed and it had nothing to do with the summer temperature. "I'm a little warm, do you mind if I turn on the AC?" The blast of cool air fanned her cheeks and she breathed deeply. Brave? Her daughter

was far more courageous than she was. How much longer would she let people believe the lies she'd told? "My
aunt and uncle definitely get the credit for the wonderful
child that Emilee's grown to be." Angelique stared out
the window at the fathomless blue sky in front of her. "I
haven't been around for the last four years of Em's life."

"You did what you had to do under the circumstances, Angie. You made sure she was safe and then took care
of yourself. Losing a husband, trying to raise a child alone
would be hard on anyone. Finding the right help, going
back to school—it was the right thing for you to do.
Now you can move forward with Emilee and the support of your family and friends and create the kind of life
you want for you and your daughter. I think that takes
amazing courage."

Angelique offered a weak smile. She wondered if Sally
would find her as brave if she knew the whole truth. If the
secret she'd kept all these years was revealed, how would
the good people of End of the Line feel about her? What
might happen to her aunt's and uncle's reputations? She
straightened, firming her resolve to do whatever she had
to in order to take care of her family. He was no longer a
part of their lives and she wanted it to stay that way.

Chapter Four

"MAMA! MAMA!" Dalton's head snapped up in reaction to Emilee's high-pitched squeal. He watched the young girl run hell-bent for her mother as she stepped from the car. He nodded his hello to Sally as she emerged, too, from the vehicle.

Angelique held her arms out to catch Emilee in a bear hug, barely giving him a second glance.

"Mama, guess what? Dalton has promised to take me on a trail ride before school starts if I have a few more riding lessons."

Angelique's gaze met his directly. "We'll have to discuss that a bit more, darling."

Big surprise. Dalton went back to tamping the fresh ground rock along the side of the new asphalt path they'd put in the last couple of days. Truth was, the little mite had at first gotten on his nerves darting from the house to the barn and back to the corral where she'd sit and watch her grandfather/uncle work with the horses. Now, he found himself chuckling at her antics, amazed by her pure energy.

"Great, I was hoping Sally would stop by. I have a couple of things I want to get her opinion on down at Clay's cabin." Rein, who'd been helping finish the path in record time, wiped his brow with a bandana. "I need to get my clipboard up at the house."

"Go on, I'll finish up with stuff here. You want me to leave this trench open for Tyler to set wiring for those lampposts?"

"Yeah." He looked over his shoulder. "I hope we can get those in next week. He and Liberty found some nice ones in a Victorian style that will look good." Rein waved at Sally. "I'll be right back."

Dalton's gaze drifted to the interaction between mother and daughter as they met up with Rein and disappeared inside the house. He noticed Sally watching him, and ducked his head as she started toward him. He didn't want to get into the topic of Angelique with her. Since the wedding, where things between them had gone badly, they'd been polite at best when in the same circles. Though it frustrated the hell out of him, Dalton figured maybe it'd get better with time.

"Hey, Dalton." Sally hooked her thumbs in her jeans. "Angelique came down to check on a horse. You know anything about that?"

"Nope." Dalton continued to smash down the rock edging. "She'll need to speak to her uncle about that."

"Right. You know," she started slowly, and he rolled his eyes knowing in his gut what was coming, "it wouldn't kill you to be nice to her." She shaded her eyes from the sun settling in the western sky.

"Sally." He slanted a warning glance to her.

She held up her palms. "Okay, okay. You two are eventually going to have to duke this out. Just sayin'."

Rein had already suggested to him that perhaps his issue with Angelique stemmed from his own abandonment issues and maybe he found fault with her for leaving her daughter with her aunt and uncle. While he couldn't deny that it bothered him on a certain level, there was far more to the story than Rein knew—a story he'd been trying to put behind him, until seeing Angelique again made it damn near impossible.

"Wow, you guys have really been busy. How far down

does this go?" Sally asked.

Glad for any topic that would side step his previous thoughts, he pointed toward the barn. "It leads from the barn here and down about fifty feet or so, where there's a slight curve leading to the other side of the pen. All total, it's probably around three to four hundred feet."

"It's beautiful. Guests will love it. I thought I heard Rein mention something about lampposts?"

"Technically, those were Liberty's idea. She thought we needed more light. I'm thinking hanging flowerpots are going to be next."

Sally nodded. "She's right. It gets black as pitch out here once you get away from that one utility pole up by the entrance."

"Guess I never noticed it much." Dalton tapped at the ground with the flat part of the garden rake.

"Jed sure would be pleased with how this has turned out." She stuffed her hands in her back pockets. "I can't hardly believe that Wyatt and Rein are married and now there's little Gracie. Jed must be smiling down on his legacy tonight."

"Yep," he responded, hoping against hope that Sally wouldn't bring up his bachelor status and Angelique in the same sentence. He had a feeling that Sally had more to do with that unplanned meeting at Dusty's a few years back than what she let on. Trouble being, how much more did she know about what happened later that night?

"I had a nice lunch with Angelique today. It sounds like she loves her new job. Keeps her busy, I guess—too busy to date, at any rate."

Dalton glanced at her and a smile curled the side of his mouth. The woman was about as subtle as a rattlesnake. He directed his gaze toward the house, willing his brother to get his butt in gear, and he breathed a sigh of relief when he saw him trotting down the porch steps.

"Hey, we've got just enough time to look at that cabinet in the cabin before dinner. We'll take the cart. What do you think of the new path?" He dropped his arm over Sally's shoulder.

She smiled. "I was just telling your brother how Jed would be pleased to see what you all have accomplished."

"Thank you, darlin', that means a lot coming from you." He planted a kiss on her temple and squeezed her shoulder. "Listen, we better hurry. Rebecca's made this beautiful roast and all of the fixings for supper. You know how she hates it when food gets cold."

"Don't plan on me for supper. I want to finish this and then I've got chores tonight."

Rein shrugged. "Suit yourself. Maybe we'll save you some. Hey, but you, Angelique, and half-pint are staying for supper, right?" Rein directed his invitation to Sally.

Sally glanced over her shoulder at Dalton. "That'll be up to Angelique. I rode in with her."

Glad for the solitude, Dalton finished his work on the path and strode to the corral butted up against the barn where they kept the rescue horses. Once Michael had proposed the idea of housing the rehabilitated equine until they were adopted, Dalton and his brothers got on board without hesitation. It seemed only natural that a ranch offering second chances to humans would do the same for animals.

He eased through the wooden gate and carefully approached the current love of his life, a dark-eyed Palomino he'd named Beauty. Dalton had been with Michael when they'd gone to pick her up at Mountain Sunrise Ranch. They'd been apprised of Beauty's story—that she was found on an abandoned farm where none of the other animals had survived. They hadn't given her much hope of being adopted due to her many health issues, but Dalton fell in love at first sight, buying her on the spot. He'd called her Beauty, as that's how he saw the determined mare and now her home was at the Kinnison ranch.

"How's my girl?" he said softly as he pulled an apple from his pocket. Stroking her warm nose, he turned his face upward and breathed in deep the calming scent of pine and hay. No matter what chaos swirled inside his brain, working outdoors and being around the horses gave him peace of mind. He'd come to realize that working with horses was a gift he possessed and by far, it was easier than dealing with humans.

He brushed the back of his hand along Beauty's face and she nickered softly. He'd learned much from working with Michael these past few weeks. The man rarely seemed conflicted about anything. Michael's astute sense of calm, his wisdom, was something that Dalton had yet to attain and as of late, the old man's beautiful niece hadn't made that goal any easier.

Beauty whinnied softly and nudged his hand as though asking for another treat.

"No more apples," he answered. "Let's get you inside. I've got a bucket of oats with your name on it, darlin'."

He heard Sally's laughter as the cart emerged from the dusky shadows of the path. Leading Beauty out of the corral, he waited as they parked the vehicle under the carport at the side of the barn.

He had to hand it to his brother and Sally. Somehow, they'd managed to remain friends even after a failed attempt at dating. It hadn't taken either of them long to realize it wasn't meant to be, and their friendship meant more.

Angelique appeared from the main house. "Hey, you two, Aunt Rebecca was wondering where the rest of her chicks are." Her smile faded when her eyes met his. "Oh, didn't see you. You coming up, Dalton?" Angelique asked.

The trio looked at him.

"Maybe later," he mumbled, hoping to avoid any confrontation.

"After the kind of day you've put in, I'd think you
could eat a bear. Aunt Rebecca won't be pleased."

Dalton sighed. "Well, I guess she's just going to have
to deal with it. I've got chores." He caught Rein's wide-
eyed surprise before he looked away and pretended to
dust off his hat.

"Shit," he heard Rein mutter softly.

Angelique's gaze held his. "I'll be up in a minute. You
two go on ahead."

Sally opened her mouth her to speak, but Rein took
her elbow and ushered her toward the house.

Angelique waited until they were up the hill before
spinning on her heel to face him. "You and I might just
as well have this out right now."

He chuckled, guessing what likely the featured topic
would be at tonight's supper table. Maybe she was right.
Maybe it was about damn time they cleared the air. Circumstances being what they were, they were bound to
run into each other here on the ranch. Damn, he hated confrontation, unless it was with his fists. "Come on,
then." He crooked his finger and led Beauty into her
stable. He took care of filling her trough with oats and
looked up to find Angelique standing in the doorway, her
arms folded across her chest.

"Well?"

He let out a short laugh, wishing he had a drink.
"Whatever you've got to say, just get it out."

"You aren't going to like it."

"Figured that." Yeah, he could be a bit abrasive at
times, but what guy wasn't? Just the same, it wasn't the
first time a woman wasn't happy with him and he didn't

think it'd be the last.

She blew out a breath and breezed past him, stopping to scratch Beauty's white spotted nose. "I'd just as soon the whole house didn't hear us."

He raised his brows. Not that they weren't likely already lined up along the front porch railing anyway. "Is this going to get violent?" He smiled, hoping to ease the look of tension in her eyes.

She turned on her heel and walked toward the back of the barn, her boots thumping the hard dirt floor in her stride. She opened the back door and let it slam behind her.

"Oh, hell yeah, this oughta be fun." Dalton blew out a sigh and followed. Stepping outside, he found her looking at the mountains. Her chin lifted slightly in defiance gave her profile a regal beauty. Hard as he tried to fight it, he swore she grew more beautiful each time he saw her. Memories slithered to the surface, snaking through his brain as he waited for her to notice his presence. Images of thick steam fogging his truck windows on that cold, rainy night, her soft lips bending to whisper that she wanted him, ran through his mind.

"Look." She swung her gaze to his. He inadvertently took a step back, reacting to her stern tone. "I don't know how to act around you. You've made it perfectly clear on more than one occasion that you regretted what happened. Or maybe you were just too drunk to remember it fully."

If he'd harbored any doubts that her recollection of that night was different than his, she'd just set the record straight. "I remember," he replied quietly.

She searched his eyes then shook her head in disbelief. "Whatever. That was a long time ago, right? And I admit, we were both maybe a little buzzed. The thing is, we've both moved on. Now I have another life—at least, I'm trying to *make* another life that doesn't include my past. So, if we could just play nice, I'd appreciate it, okay?" Having said her piece, she started around him.

He caught her arm. "What about Emilee?"

Her gaze snapped to his and pure fear flashed in her eyes. He dropped his hold as though she was on fire. Her expression eased some, but she looked away. He'd heard bits and pieces—mostly rumors—that her marriage hadn't been stellar, that she'd been in an abusive relationship. "What are we going to do about the promise I made to her about the trail ride?"

Her gaze, softer now, looked up at him, but she held her ground. "We aren't going to do anything. I'll need to think about it, like I told her."

"Fair enough, and while you're at it, think on this. There may be one or two things about that night I don't remember too well." He touched her chin and forced her gaze to his. Those dark eyes bore into his sorry excuse for a soul. He knew he didn't deserve someone like her, but that didn't make things any easier in the middle of the night. "I must have said something that hurt you enough to make you detest me like you do."

She jerked her arm from his grasp. "I don't detest you, Dalton. I just don't see any possible future with you. To be honest, I'm not sure I ever did. I admit, I'm as much to blame for what happened that night. It was careless and stupid."

"It might have been careless, might have been many things, but stupid wasn't one of them."

"I'm surprised you felt anything. Figured as much time as you spent at Dusty's that day…." She shook her head and looked away.

That stung, and maybe he deserved it. He could refute it, but it was true—he'd been there most of the afternoon. Still, if darts were being thrown, it would be easy to pin her with why she'd given up her daughter for the past four years to be raised by someone else. Maybe there was more to the story, maybe not. He'd known one woman who hadn't thought one red hot damn about abandoning her children. But that wasn't what challenged him. It was her disbelief in his memory. Because he'd sure as hell remembered that night—remembered her sighs, the way her hands fisted in his hair as she called out his name. "That's not at all how I remember it." He took a step closer, knowing he risked bodily injury. "In fact, I *felt* everything in vivid detail. And so, did you, let's be truthful about that, shall we?"

Her expression remained stoic. "Well, I guess we can both agree that it was a mistake. And as long as we're being truthful, until that night—when I seduced you, by the way—you never knew I existed."

He couldn't deny that either. Hell, when he'd seen her with Sally at Dusty's that night, he'd not recognized her. Only after she stormed out and Sally chewed him a new one did he realize who she was. She blamed him for embarrassing her. Hell, he blamed himself, which is why he'd apologized. Had he planned on what happened between them? No, but he couldn't deny she'd put his life in a tailspin that night. Just before she went back to Chicago and got married. One last fling, he figured. He'd tried to shrug it off, to pretend he hadn't burned for her weeks after she'd gone.

But that was then, and this was now. Whatever he had stuck in his craw about her, he'd have to battle through, which shouldn't be too difficult since it seemed abundantly clear that she wanted even less to do with him than he originally thought. She had, however, sparked a curiosity. Or *fuck,* maybe he just saw it as a personal challenge. Without a trace of alcohol in his system, he wondered if her lips would taste as sweet as he remembered. Tossing good sense aside, he moved closer, forcing her back against the barn until she couldn't escape. He braced one arm above her and looked down at the fire dancing in her defiant gaze, almost daring him to make a move.

So, he did.

She pushed her fists against his chest and he grabbed them, lifting them above her head as he closed in, taking his fill of that sweet mouth. She may have wanted to tell him to go to hell, but her body responded differently. Kiss for fiery kiss, she met his mouth until she broke free of his grasp and held his head, keeping his mouth to hers. He wasn't sure if the moan he heard was his or hers.

Dalton was ready to take this to a nice soft patch of hay when she ducked away from him. "No."

"No?" He chuckled. "That sure as hell didn't feel like no."

"I wish you hadn't done that."

"It was a kiss, Angel, nothing more. And, by the way, you participated fully."

Her eyes met his. "Exactly, and that's why it won't happen again." She whirled on her heel and headed toward the house.

He whipped off his hat and shook his head. Frustrated in more ways than one, he strode back into the barn. Snatching a horsewhip from the wall, he used it to knock a bottle of Jack Daniels he kept hidden in the rafters. Settling in a hay bale, he uncapped the bottle and took a long pull from it. His eyes watered as the liquid fire slid down his parched throat.

A soft whinny brought his head up and he realized that Beauty had managed to jimmy the latch on her stall. She dipped her head and nuzzled his hand holding the bottle, shaking her blonde mane in protest.

"Yeah, probably not the best medicine for frustration."

The memory of Rein's words rolled over him, dredging up guilt as he eyed the half-empty bottle in his hand. He had his drinking under control, *didn't he?* It was everything else going on that made it seem like he wasn't together. He took another drink, capped the bottle, and stuffed it in his jacket. Her scent lingered in his mind. Her lips tasted just as he'd remembered. No great consolation.

He raked his hand through his hair and, heaving a sigh, led Beauty back to her stall, taking care this time to secure the latch. Hearing the sound of a car starting up, he stepped out of the barn and watched the taillights of Angelique's car disappear as she turned onto the highway.

Not the least bit hungry or ready to face the questions his family was likely to pepper him with, he retreated to his cabin, fixed himself a sandwich, and then showered, letting the hot water ease the tensions of the day. Tossing the towel aside, he turned off the bathroom light and immersed himself into darkness.

He walked over to the window and opened it, letting the mountain's night breeze cool his body. Tearing back the comforter, he dropped onto the sheets, staring at the moonlight streaked across his ceiling. Thoughts of her knotted his stomach. Why should it matter what she thought of him? Even now, with one simple phone call, he could enlist the help of any one of a dozen women who'd happily help him ease his frustration.

Maybe Angelique was right. Maybe that night in the school lot had been a mistake. It wasn't the first choice he'd made in his life that had gone awry. But if it was a mistake, then why had it taken him weeks, months to stop thinking of her every damn second of the day? He rubbed his hand over his chest, still cool and damp from his shower. A gentle breeze fluttered the curtains, causing the gooseflesh to rise on his body. He remembered how she'd touched him, her hands exploring, tentative, yet without fear. Remembered how she'd crawled onto his lap, taken him deep inside her, how their bodies rocked in tandem....

His body tightened. Relinquishing his control to the memory of her sweet sighs, self-made pleasure ripped through his body, but there was no satisfaction. He took a deep breath and gazed at the ceiling fan spinning above him. No less tense, he dropped his feet to the floor and stood in front of the window, hands braced on the frame as he let the chilly mountain air cool his fevered body. She wanted to be "friends." As though nothing had happened to possibly change that.

He should drop it. Give her what she wants. But her kiss tonight, the way she responded to him, stuck in his brain. He'd seen the fear on her face. Was it only the past, or something else? Regardless, if she just wanted to be friends, why the hell would she kiss him like her life depended on it? It left him more than curious. It left him wanting—more than just a roll in the hay. He was determined to find a way to get to the truth of whether that night meant anything at all to her. Maybe then, he could move on with his life.

Angelique handed her aunt another Dutch apple pie to add to the several being boxed to take to the Kinnison barbecue that night. Emilee had pleaded to go with her grandpa to help him with chores before the guests began to arrive.

"What time is Sally stopping by to pick you up?" Her aunt asked as she carefully arranged the pies so they wouldn't overlap in the shallow cardboard tray.

"Around four, unless you need her to come earlier?" Angelique sampled the potato salad, adding more pepper to it. This was her kind of heaven, cooking with her aunt in this old country kitchen. She knew where everything was kept, knew how the scorch mark on the kitchen Formica came to be during a trial run of baking her first cookies alone.

"Emilee seems to enjoy helping out with the baby and helping with the horses," her aunt remarked, tearing off another piece of foil to cover another pie.

Angelique smiled as she spooned her salad into large tubs for ease in transporting. "You know how she loves horses."

"She mentioned that Dalton is teaching her how to ride. He seems to have taken a shine to her."

Angelique had been well aware of how much her daughter spoke about Dalton. While she appreciated his kindness, she couldn't help but wonder about his sudden change of heart with children. A self-proclaimed bachelor and proud of it, children had always been more of something to be tolerated. Maybe being an uncle had changed his perspective. In the past few days since their discussion, she'd noticed via Emilee how much more present he seemed to be to her—taking time to teach her to ride, how to tie various knots in a rope, mucking stalls, showing her how to identify wildflowers from poisonous plants. Guilt more than anything else pushed the next words from her mouth. "Well, school will be starting in a few weeks. I'm not certain it's best for her to be spending so much time in Dalton's company."

Her aunt offered no response and for a few moments, they worked in amiable silence. Angelique finished loading the salad into the cooler and shut the lid. "There, I think we're about ready. Was there anything else?"

Her aunt spoke as she continued her task of wrapping another pie. "When are you going to tell that boy the truth?"

Angelique's heart faltered. "What boy?"

Her aunt's steady gaze looked up to meet hers. "Dalton Kinnison."

"I don't know what you mean."

Rebecca dropped her fist holding the hand towel against the countertop. Her eyes pinned Angelique where she stood. "I mean when do you plan to tell him who Emilee's real father is?"

Unable to speak, she lowered herself to a nearby breakfast stool—the same one she used to climb up and prop her knees on so she could watch her aunt put together her pies. "How did you know?"

Rebecca's gaze softened. "I didn't, not until this moment. I've seen similarities in her behavior—little things. But those eyes, their color, and her smile—they're unmistakably Dalton's."

Angelique covered her face, unwilling to acknowledge the lie she'd kept hidden for so long. She looked up at her aunt and tried to hold the desperation inside her at bay. "You must promise me that you'll not breathe a word of this to anyone—not even Uncle Michael."

Her aunt frowned at the request, but after a moment, she pulled up another stool and sat across from her, waiting for an explanation. "If you truly feel that's what's best, I will honor that for now." Her hand covered Angelique's. "I know it couldn't have been easy for you. I didn't want to press you to tell me everything that you went through. But one day Emilee's going to reach an age—very soon—when she'll want to know more about her father. You've fabricated this story of him as a war hero, who died serving his country. What will you tell her when she asks to see pictures of him and realizes that she doesn't look like him at all?"

She pulled away and twisted her fingers together in her lap. "I was just trying to get us on our feet. Start a new life." Angelique looked down at her hand where her wedding band used to be. "I'd planned to explain it to her one day when she was older and able to understand."

"Why don't you tell me everything? Help me to understand what happened; why you couldn't tell us the real reason you wanted Emilee far away from Chicago."

Taking a fortifying breath, she stared out the kitchen window, its bright yellow gingham curtains pulled back to reveal the open field beyond. "That night with Dalton," she began. "I knew when I got back to Chicago that something was different. I suspected I was pregnant and took one of those early tests that proved my suspicions were true."

"What did Anthony say?" Rebecca asked.

Angelique shook her head. "I didn't tell him at first. I honestly didn't know whose baby it was. I only knew that Tony, with all his faults, said he loved me and wanted to marry me. It was clear back then that Dalton didn't want to be tied down." She glanced at her aunt's concerned face. "I thought if we got married, if Tony and I could start a family, a home, maybe it would give him a new purpose."

"A fresh start?" her aunt offered.

"Yes. I hoped it would help. Give him incentive, pull him out of the depression he seemed to be in." She stared off into space, thinking back to those tumultuous days, never knowing what mood he'd be in when she came home from work, or if he'd be there at all. "For a while he was better. He acknowledged his angry times, tried to do better. The hitting stopped—" Tears welled in her eyes. She felt her aunt's hand squeeze hers.

"Why didn't you come home? Ask us for help?"

Angelique pressed her lips together, summoning the courage to continue. Even now, she questioned her choices. Her state of mind at that time wanted to believe she could change him. "If I could just show him that he was loved, that someone cared, maybe he'd change." She looked up searching her aunt's sorrowful gaze.

"Oh, child." Her aunt touched her cheek and she pressed on, wanting to free the lies, to get out everything she'd bottled up inside her all this time.

"One day I had to work late at the restaurant. I'd left Emilee with a woman down the hall—a nice woman who kept giving me flyers and telling me there were people who could help me in my situation." She closed her eyes, remembering the day. "It was after dark. My shift was to end at five, but the woman on nightshift called in sick. I had a chance for a little overtime and so I stayed until they could find a replacement.

"I walked out an hour later, hurrying to get to the corner stop before the next bus, and saw Tony's car sitting in the parking lot. He revved the motor and leaned out the window. His eyes were wide and glassy, his grin like a crazy man.

'Hey, you're late,' he said. 'That woman almost wouldn't let me pick up Emilee tonight. What the fuck? I want you to find a new babysitter. Dammit, it's always something with you isn't it?'

"He wasn't making sense and I questioned getting in the car, but what choice did I have?"

'Could you be any slower,' he said, revving the motor as I walked around the car. 'Come on, I'm hungry and we need beer. Get the fuck in the car.'

She looked down at her hands, wondering if she could have done anything different. "I saw Emilee in the back seat and pleaded with him to let me take her out, that I'd go on home and get dinner started while he did his beer run. I barely had my hand on the door handle when he screamed, 'Fuck this' and threw the car in reverse, dragging me with him until I yelled loud enough that people began gathering at the restaurant window. He stopped suddenly and I was scared that he'd hurt Emilee. He leaned across the front seat and glared at me.

'Get in now, bitch, or you'll never see your brat again. "He pushed open the passenger door. I got in. I had no choice. I had no choice," she heard herself say in the silence of the old kitchen.

"I'm so sorry you went through this, Angelique." Her aunt brushed a soothing hand down her hair.

"Oh, it got worse. He tore out of the parking lot and into traffic. I remember tires squealing, horns honking, but I didn't dare tell him to slow down. He was out of control. He pulled into a corner gas station. He actually smiled as he took the keys from the ignition and held out his hand. 'I need money.' Emilee started to whimper and I knew it was past her suppertime. I gave him everything in my apron."

As though in a trance, she remembered him slamming the door, jarring her to her senses. "I looked around but most things were closed. The neighborhood was run down and I was too scared to try to find help, afraid that it might be worse. He came out a few minutes later, a six-pack under his arm and a gun in his hand. He stopped in front of the car and fired back at the store. I couldn't see what happened. Gas pumps blocked my view. Then he was in the car, tossing the beer in my lap and the gun on the seat."

Aunt Rebecca gasped in horror, covering her mouth.

"It discharged and the bullet sliced through the side of my foot. I was screaming, Emilee was crying. He was yelling for us to stop, banging his hand against the wheel. I pulled my seat belt on as he started the car and prayed that Emilee was secure. He flew through traffic and soon I heard sirens. He cursed, and drove faster, trying to out-run the police. I was helpless to do anything but hang on. He tried to get around a car, turning the wheel too far, and he couldn't recover. The car went airborne, landing nose first on an embankment. The back end slammed to a rest, shattering the back window. I didn't remember anything else until I woke up in the hospital."

Tears stained Angelique's face and she realized that her knuckles were white, gripping her aunt's hand. "When I came to in the hospital, they told me that Tony had wounded the clerk at the gas station in the robbery. Aside from the beer, he'd taken money and, worse, they'd found a packet of cocaine in his jeans." She released a breath to try to lessen the tightness in her chest. "They told me Emilee was fine, but said it was only our seat belts that saved us. I was terrified what might happen to Emilee. That's why I called you. The woman who took care of Emilee found me a lawyer who handles domestic abuse cases—that's how she was able to be turned over into your care."

She looked at her aunt. "I felt like such a failure. I was in no shape to care for a child. I had no idea what to do, what would come next." She stood then and crossed her arms over her chest, walking to the window. "It took weeks…months, for me to heal. I stayed with Mrs. Harrison, went to group sessions for women like me who'd been in abusive situations. It was a start. But there was still Tony. It came to light that he'd been involved with drugs—not only using but also selling. I knew he'd used occasionally, but only once or twice did he do so at home. I agreed to testify against him, give them names of people he'd mentioned when he'd go drinking. I offered my lawyer an account of Tony's violent behavior, what I knew about his using and it wasn't difficult to obtain a divorce. I was able to have you come get Emilee, because Tony never asked about her. He never knew that I hadn't listed him as the father."

A car horn sounded outside and, wiping her face, she

looked back at her aunt.

"You are a brave woman, Angelique." She walked over and wrapped her arms around her. "I had no idea that you'd been through so much."

"I-I didn't want to end up like my mother," she said, her voice breaking as fresh tears flowed against her aunt's cotton dress.

Aunt Rebecca stroked the back of her head, offering soothing words of comfort, quieting Angelique's soul as she'd done so often in the past.

"It's all behind you now, sweetheart. And your courage and love for Emilee is the reason for your accomplishments. No one could want for a better mother. She's a lucky little girl." Rebecca held her at arm's length. "We're here for you as always. And we're so proud of you, Angelique. So very proud."

She sniffed, wiping her face once more. "Sally's going to wonder what's keeping us." She managed a wobbly smile.

Rebecca took her chin in her hand. "Do you have feelings for Dalton?"

Searching her aunt's gaze, she shrugged. "I don't know, maybe. He rejected me once before. Tony deceived me and it almost cost Emilee and me our lives. Maybe I need to stand on my own for a while. Besides, it seems Dalton still has an issue with drinking and I can't afford to be messed up with someone like that again. I guess if I've learned nothing else, it's that I can't save someone who doesn't want to be saved, no matter how much I love them. I need to take care of me and Emilee for now."

Rebecca nodded. But even as her aunt pulled her into another embrace, Angelique knew that her feelings for Dalton were as strong as they ever were. That kiss they'd shared behind the barn and the number of times she'd replayed it in her head was undisputable evidence. How would he react to the knowledge that Emilee was his? She wasn't about to box him in with obligations—not after all this time. She and Emilee were just fine on their own, and when she saved enough to find a place—well, she'd decide then what was best for the two of them.

Chapter Five

HE WAS DAMN TIRED OF thinking about her and he'd be double-damned if he was going to stick around. He was a stupid-ass fool for thinking that kiss meant anything, and he had paid for it every night this week. He was hungry for more and she'd given him the decree that it wouldn't happen again. Which was why he'd decided to head up to the cabin to do a little fishing this weekend. It was a helluva lot better than sitting around here tormenting himself with having to keep his distance.

"Hey, where're you headed?" Rein asked, walking down from the back of the house where he'd delivered wood for the fire pit. He swiped the wood chips off the front of his shirt, waiting for an answer. Dalton figured he wasn't going to like it.

Dalton hefted his metal cooler into the back of the truck. His tackle box, rod, and assorted gear followed. "Heading up to the cabin. Want to get in a little fishing before the weather turns."

Rein slipped off his hat and scratched the top of his head, causing his sandy brown hair to stand on end. "You forget we have a barbecue tonight and half the town is invited?"

"Nope." Dalton snapped his rifle into the rack behind the jump seat.

Rein grinned. "Gonna shoot them fish?"

Dalton tossed him a look. "Like I have to remind you about the bears up there?"

"Ok, fair enough." Rein nodded. "Plan on being back before supper?"

"Nope," he answered again, and lifted a box of food and cleaning supplies in the back.

Rein held out his arms, confusion etched on his face. "Hey we've had a lot of people say they were coming. It's kind of our grand opening. Clay's supposed to arrive, and— "

Dalton swung his gaze around and looked at his brother. "*Everyone* is exactly why I don't plan to be around. You, Wyatt, Aimee, and Liberty can handle everything just fine." He slung his old duffel bag on the truck, followed by a jug of kerosene and some fresh towels. "I'll have my cell phone, but you know how sketchy the signal can be up there. Plan to bring back some walleye and make sure the cabin's shut down for the winter." He dug in his pocket, retrieving his keys.

"Wait a minute," Rein said. "It's because *she's* going to be here, isn't it?" He narrowed his eyes on Dalton.

He flipped his ball cap around on his head and leaned against the truck, crossing his arms over his chest. He slid his sunglasses over his eyes. "Let this go, Rein. I don't have the time or energy for it."

"Something's eating you about her. And for the record, it appears that I'm not the only one who needs to let go." Rein pointed his finger at him.

Dalton blew out an impatient sigh. "It's not what you think. Even if I was interested—which I'm not," he lied. "She sure the hell isn't. Done. Conversation over." He turned, grabbing the door handle, hoping that Rein would drop it.

"And you've talked to her about this?"

Dalton jerked open the driver's door. "Yes, as a matter of fact, we did have a talk." He crooked his fingers for emphasis and wished he'd left just a little earlier to avoid this interrogation.

"And?" Rein asked.

Belligerent bastard, that is.

Dalton swiped his hand over his mouth and eyed his brother. Angelique's comments about his drinking and trying to forget her past still stung when he thought about them, which was every damn time he thought about her. "She thinks I drink too much." He held up his hand to stop Rein's response. "And I know that you and Wyatt feel the same. Hell, half the county probably feels I drink too much." Anger simmered just below the surface. He needed to get out of there before he said something he'd surely regret.

"Dalton," Rein's voice was calm, much calmer than Dalton felt. "You do remember her mom, don't you? Angelique grew up having to care for an alcoholic mother."

He waited patiently for Rein to finish. "You know, I understand that, but just because her mom was a drunk doesn't mean that I am."

Rein held up his hands. "I never…we *never* said nor do we believe that you're a drunk. I've told you before I get concerned because drinking seems to be how you handle your problems."

"And you think I can't control it?"

Rein shook his head. "I didn't say that."

"You didn't have to." Dalton climbed in the cab. "I'll be back on Sunday. And for the record. there's no beer in the truck."

"Dalton, come on, man."

However, the roar of his truck swallowed Rein's words. He glanced at the rearview mirror once and saw Rein shaking his head. Fine. A couple of days would give them both a little time to cool down.

He stopped at the Git–n–Go to pick up a few things, tempted when he walked past the cooler to add a six-

ck under his arm. Pausing, he eyed the frosty bottles.
"Screw it," he muttered and snagged the beer. If he wanted to relax with a beer or two, that was damn well his own business.

A few moments later, he surfed through several stations until he found one that came in clear as he zoomed along the winding two-lane road. He watched civilization disappear, smiling as he hummed along with the country music tunes, the summer breeze whipping through the open windows of his truck. No distractions. No drama. Just blessed solitude, and a little fishing for two glorious days.

Three hours, two snakes, and several cobwebs later, Dalton surveyed the open-room cabin, pleased with how few critters had actually taken up residence. He lit a fire in the stone fireplace, then dug through the cabinets and filled the kerosene lamps with oil. The ice he'd brought would last a day or two, at least. Bread, peanut butter, and some fruit would sustain him if fishing proved unsuccessful. Popping off the cap of one of the longneck beers, he walked out and stood on the front porch. Taking a long pull, he savored the quiet and looked for evidence that he might be sharing the area with the forest's permanent residents. He noted deep gouges on the trunks of one or two trees likely made by antlers, reminding him of times when he'd wake early enough to watch the deer amble across the dirt road they'd hewn through the forest.

He inhaled the familiar comforting scent of warm wood and pine, letting go the tension that had been building inside him. Peering up at the sky through the sentinel of tall pine surrounding the cabin, he noticed dark, black clouds rolling in from the northwest. They could use the rain as long as lightning didn't come with it. He took a pull of his beer and started back inside when he heard a soft rustle. Turning on his heel, he stepped to the edge of the porch. He scanned his surroundings, his eyes and ears attentive as they searched in the waning light of the pre-storm dimness. The hair on the back of his neck stood on end as his eyes connected with the gaze of a Great White owl, feathers the color of virgin snow. The bird hooted once as if in greeting.

Dalton's shoulders relaxed and he lifted his empty bottle in salute to the animal. The realization that he'd seen the bird on occasion soaring around the ranch didn't fully hit him until a moment later. The bottle weighed like a heavy stone as he lowered his hand. He held the large owl's luminous golden eyes. Not one to readily adhere to the superstitious lore that Michael Greyfeather often spoke of, he couldn't deny the strange feeling that this owl being here was just a coincidence.

A heartbeat later, the bird spread its majestic wings and soared up through the trees, disappearing as quickly as it had appeared. According to an old Indian belief, the Great Owl's appearance was sign of an impending storm. He eyed the darkening clouds and, glancing at the bottle, poured out the remainder over the side of the porch. A shrill ring startled him and he dug in his pocket, amazed that he even had a signal.

"Hey, it's Wyatt. Rein told me you'd headed up to the cabin. Just checking to see if you've got everything you need."

Dalton smiled, knowing that Wyatt would never come right out and ask if he was okay. "I'm good. Just needed some time. Thought I'd make sure the cabin was closed up and ready for winter."

"Probably a good idea. Rein also mentioned that you plan on fishing?"

He stepped to the edge of the porch and leaned on the railing. He wasn't the only one fishing, apparently. "Thought about it, yeah."

"Just checked the weather. Looks like a thunderstorm might be heading in. Hopefully, the roof won't leak. God knows it's been so dry we can use the rain, though."

"I checked everything over when I got here. Things are just fine." He toed the old floorboards with his boot. "Sorry I won't be at the BBQ. But you've got plenty of help."

"It's still early enough in the day. You could still change your mind."

Dalton's mouth curved in a half smile. "Probably not." Wanting to divert from discussing the reasons why he'd chosen his impromptu sabbatical, he brought up the recent odd sighting. "Hey, do you remember seeing this huge white owl hanging out around the ranch?"

Wyatt's chuckle emitted from the other end of the line. "Yeah, in fact, I do, but not in a while. Why, have you seen it?"

"It just flew over a few minutes ago. Landed on a tree and I swear to God the damn thing just stared at me."

"Yeah. You know what Michael says. It's a sign of an unexpected storm about to blow in."

Dalton looked up at the ever-darkening sky. "Yeah, I did notice the storm clouds."

Wyatt cleared his throat. "Rein tells me the reason you high-tailed it up there had something to do with Angelique Juarez."

"Rein is full of shit." Dalton scowled, cataloging a reminder to take care of Rein when he got back.

"Just like another brother I know," Wyatt responded. "I couldn't help but overhear a little of your discussion with Angelique behind the barn."

"Jesus. Can't a guy have any privacy? And you wonder why I had to come up here?"

"Simmer down. I happened to be taking a ripe diaper out to the trash bin. I happened to hear part of the conversation, is all. It's not really any of my business."

"Damn straight, it's not," Dalton said. "Hey, gotta go. I want to go catch my dinner before the rain."

"Okay, okay, take it easy."

"I'll see you sometime tomorrow." Dalton picked up his tackle box, checking his lures. "Oh, and hey, I'd appreciate it if you wouldn't mention to anyone, especially Aimee, what you accidentally overheard."

"Got it. And little brother, one more thing about that owl you spotted?"

"Yeah?" Dalton sighed.

"I was visited by it once. Just before Aimee breezed into my life."

Dalton rolled his eyes upward. "Your point?"

Wyatt let out a sigh. "Just that maybe the storms can be us fighting the changes in life, not necessarily relating to the weather."

"Thanks, *Gandhi*," Dalton said with a chuckle. "I'll keep that in mind. His smile faded as his gaze landed on the Great White owl perched on a nearby branch, studying him.

"You're an ass, you know that, right?" Wyatt said.

Dalton held the owl's unblinking eyes. "So, I've been told...many times."

"So, have you found out any more about this Clay Saunders?" Angelique directed the question to Sally as they drove the back roads to the Kinnison BBQ. She glanced in the backseat and saw Aunt Rebecca staring out of the window as though deep in thought. No doubt. Angelique had unleashed on her everything that she'd kept bottled up for so long. And while sharing it lifted a weight that Angelique had carried forever, it seemed, the confession was now in her aunt's heart. Processing it all would take time. As to how she felt about Dalton or the question of whether to tell him about Emilee—that remained a quandary.

"Hank is supposed to be bringing him to the ranch to help him get settled in. I guess having the BBQ was timed perfectly in terms of him meeting a lot of folks from the community." Sally kept her eyes on the road.

"I guess he's probably cute?" Angelique let the comment roll off her tongue, mostly to gauge Sally's reaction. "I thought I heard Clay was a strapping Texas cowboy." She caught her friend's furrowed brow.

"Yeah," Sally said cautiously. "Considering he's a former football player, probably tan from spending time outdoors. Odds are good." She turned to look at her. "Are you interested?"

"Me? Heavens, no!" Angelique responded. "I was curious if you might be."

"I'm going to have enough on my plate this summer with shepherding those kids on a trail ride." Sally said. "Still, a girl can look, can't she? Say, speaking of being curious, you never did spill about what you and Dalton talked about the other night."

"It wasn't important." Angelique glanced at Sally, then focused on the road.

"Really?" Sally asked. "Odd, he's apparently not going to be around this weekend. I thought maybe it might have had something to do with your talk." She crooked her fingers for emphasis.

Angelique kept her gaze forward, feeling her aunt's eyes boring into the back of her head. She was partly relieved that she wouldn't have to face him and yet selfish as it was, a slap of guilt smacked her brain. What was the point in telling him the truth about Emilee—then or now? What was done was done. Choices had been made.

"Angelique?" Sally's voice broke through her thoughts. "Did you hear what I said?"

She looked at Sally, who'd pushed hard for her to get to know Dalton. She hadn't even told Sally about that night. Angelique squared her shoulders. "Yes, I did. I'd think he'd want to be there to celebrate the grand opening with his brothers."

Sally turned the car down the long entrance to the Kinnison ranch. "Well, you know how Dalton hates crowds, though it puzzles me that he'd miss greeting Clay." She pulled into the grassy area at the side of the house corded off for parking.

Angelique smiled as she saw Emilee tugging her grandfather's hand as they walked to meet them at the car. Waiting no longer, she released his hand and flew into Angelique's arms.

"I helped Grandpa with chores, then Rein let me put a log on the fire pit and I helped feed Gracie her bottle because Aimee says she's always hungry."

Angelique watched her little girl's dark amber eyes dance with excitement. She lived life to the fullest—a "dancing rainbow," her grandfather called her. It was healing balm to Angelique's soul to see her happy, carefree, as a child should be, assured in knowing how much she is loved.

"Do you need some help, Grandma?" Emilee wiggled free, her red cowboy boots hitting the solid earth.

"Sure, baby girl, you can carry the basket to the kitchen for me. Michael, there's another box of pies in the trunk, would you get those for me?"

Kinnison gatherings, Angelique knew from experience, were anything but subdued. Wyatt's and Aimee's wedding was the last assemblage of half the town. Aimee had bonded with Emilee during the winter storm that had stranded Aimee and her second-grade class at the ranch. The event, now legendary in the community, served as a pivotal turning point in Wyatt's life, and

ultimately led to their engagement. Aimee had wanted
Emilee to be flower girl and with two brothers, needed
an additional bridesmaid, it seemed logical to ask Angelique to be involved as Emilee's mother.

Today, however, the backyard appeared to be a giant
reunion. Rectangular picnic tables with red and white
checked tablecloths provided seating for hungry guests.
Wyatt was hard at work at the grill, handing off trays of
smoked ribs and burgers to Liberty and Rein who were
busily staging the food tables.

Aimee waved at her and Sally as she emerged from
the kitchen holding a sack of buns in one hand and baby
Grace snuggled against her front in a baby carrier.

Angelique hurried up to the deck and took the buns
from Aimee. "Where do these go?"

Aimee smiled, but her face showed her weariness.
"Anywhere on that long table is fine. There should be a
basket there somewhere, and we need to make room for
Rebecca's pies. They look amazing. I may skip the burgers and go right for dessert.

Wyatt, holding a long spatula in his mitt-covered
hand, snaked his free arm around his wife's waist, dropping a kiss on her temple and Gracie's tiny head. "Ladies."
He nodded to Angelique, taking the buns and tossing
them over the crowd to Rein. Wyatt tossed a smile over
his shoulder as he caught the bag with precision.

"Doesn't look like he has a prayer when it comes to
that baby girl," Sally said. "She's already got him wrapped
around her tiny little fingers."

Angelique reached over to peek at the dozing child.

"I've never seen him like this. It's a side of him that
mystifies me still." Aimee grinned.

Liberty joined them as they stood on the deck ogling
little Gracie June. "I can't wait to see how he deals with
her first date." She smiled and kissed Aimee's forehead.

"Get prepared for that one."

Aimee nodded. "Don't think I haven't thought about it."

"Hey," Liberty continued. "Rein said that Hank just called. He and Clay Saunders just got to town. They should be here in a few minutes."

Rein trotted up the deck steps behind his wife and wrapped an arm around her. "You think I could talk you into making more of that bubble concoction for the kids? They're plowing right through the gallon you made."

"So, Clay and Hank are on their way?" Sally asked. "Is there anything we should do to make things any easier for him?"

Rein shook his head. "Clay's been very clear that he wants no special treatment. He gets by with his prosthetic and a cane. Hanks says he gets tired fast, but part of that might be a little depression."

Sally nodded. "I can understand that part. Dad had days when he was depressed."

"I think we just need to give him some space. Let him get used to things around here, then maybe ease him into helping out each day." He looked over Liberty's shoulder through the large paned windows of the great room. "Speaking of, they're here. Excuse me, ladies. I'll go see to our guest."

Angelique stood in awe, once again struck with how Jed Kinnison's vision of making this ranch a place of healing and second chances. In spite of everything, the ranch in its idyllic, rustic setting embodied a sense of calm that welcomed the lost.

She felt a hand on her shoulder and turned to find her Uncle Mike. "The suggestion you made about Champion's leg worked well. Would you like to see him?"

"Sure." Angelique followed him around the side of the house, past the woodworking shop and into the barn.

The scent of warm, sweet hay tickled her nose. Beauty, Dalton's rescue horse—a lovely Palomino—raised her head as though hoping to see him. She stopped to scratch the brown-eyed horse's nose. "He'll be back tomorrow, girl," she said soothingly.

"The salve you placed on his knee has taken the swelling down." Michael knelt by a chestnut stallion that he'd chosen to call Champion. Left for dead on an abandoned farm, likely due to foreclosure, the horse had sustained an eye injury and other various issues due to neglect. Under the care of the Mountain Sunrise Ranch, Champion was nearly ready to be adopted by a forever family who would agree to care for, protect, and respect the animal for the rest of its natural life. Her uncle, however, had taken a particular interest in this horse.

"He's a little rough around the edges. But in here" —he tapped his chest—"beats the heart of a champion. He's a good horse—dependable and strong despite his challenges. Very gentle and loving. He just needed someone to give him a chance. Show him a little love."

Angelique drew her hand down the side of the horse's face, noting a glint of mischief in his warm, brown eyes. She glanced at her uncle, a niggling sense that he wasn't just talking about the horse. "Have you been talking to Aunt Rebecca?" She continued to brush her hand over the horse, receiving a gentle nudge when she paused.

"Your aunt is a wise woman. I'm old enough to appreciate that," he said. Though she had no idea how much her aunt had shared, she was certain that something about Dalton had come up—at least, in part.

"I'd like to handle my own relationships. When and if I choose to have them." She looked at her uncle.

He shrugged and offered an apple to Champion. "You have always been independent, Angelique. While you could have grown up a victim of your circumstances, blamed the world, or given up, you persevered and did well for yourself and your daughter."

She blinked away the tears threatening to spill over. "Thank you, Uncle Mike. That means so much coming from you."

He sat down on a bale of hay, and she noted the time it took him to do so. He was no longer the tougher-than-steel man she remembered as a child, and while he wasn't frail, he moved a bit slower these days. Hell, she moved slower these days. Still, she had a feeling he was gearing up. This conversation wasn't over.

"I've known Dalton Kinnison since he was in his teens—bitter, broken almost beyond repair after his mother left Jed and those boys. He'd barely lived here a year and had to deal with all the small-town tongue wagging speculating on the reasons for his mother's and father's problems. I imagine it wasn't easy." He waved his hand. "Don't get me wrong, Jed did an incredible job with those boys, all three of them. But when he died, they were barely out of college. Another devastating loss. Now his brothers have wives, and they're starting families. I imagine he must feel a little displaced right about now."

She listened and understood how Dalton could feel as he did—if her uncle was correct, of course. But what responsibility did she have in all of this? "He's been through a great deal. Fortunately, he's had his brothers and the ranch to fall back on."

Michael nodded. "True, up to a few months ago when everything about this ranch as he knew it started to change."

"Life changes. You of all people should know that. Mine did. I had to adapt, survive. Decide what I wanted," Angelique replied. She folded her arms over her chest and stood at the barn entrance looking out over the wide-open prairie and the mountain range on the horizon.

"And do you know what you want?" her uncle asked.

"Not yet, not fully, anyway, but I'm working on it." She looked at him. "Do you mind telling me where you're going with this?"

"Maybe you have more in common than you think with Dalton. Seems neither of you has found what you want."

"Do you remember the part where I said I'd handle my own relationships?"

"Your aunt tells me that you may have feelings for Dalton."

Angelique sighed. She knew they meant well. "Uncle Mike," she warned gently.

He slapped both hands over his knees. "May I be candid?"

She chuckled. As if she could stop him. "Please, go ahead."

"If nothing else, you are both going to be around each other a great deal. And for the sake of us all, you're going to have to find some way of developing a friendly existence around him. Everyone has felt the tension."

"Everyone?" Angelique leveled him a skeptical look.

"Emilee asked me if you were angry with Dalton."

Her memory shot back to the day Grace was born and the talk they'd had on the way home that night. "Okay. I'll talk to him."

"I heard he's gone up to the Kinnison cabin this weekend. Claimed he hates crowds. My bet is it's because you were going to be here."

"That's ridiculous." Yet even as she refuted the notion, the explosive kiss they'd shared scorched her memory.

"Only one way to find out." Michael shrugged.

Angelique sighed. "I can't just go traipsing after Dalton."

"Who said anything about going after him? I'm only suggesting that you talk out whatever it is between the two of you so the rest of us don't have to deal with it every time you're in the same vicinity. It's bad juju for the animals, not to mention little Emilee."

She let her hands drop to her sides. "Please, don't hold back." She chewed the corner of her lip. "Okay, maybe I've been behaving badly around him. He gets on my nerves. Sometimes I think on purpose. I didn't realize it was that noticeable."

"Only to half the town."

"May I borrow your truck? I can ask Sally if she'd mind taking you home. I might be rather late."

Michael fished in his pocket and handed her the keys.

At that moment, Aunt Rebecca peeked inside the barn. She held a picnic basket. "Sally already agreed to take us home."

"Seriously?" she said. "Have we really drummed up that much tension around here?"

Her aunt handed the basket over, then Angelique's purse and jacket.

"Let's just say that any relationship needs to hash things out from time to time."

Angelique plucked the jacket from her aunt's offered hand. "May I remind you that there is no *relationship* between Dalton and me?"

Her uncle stood and put his arm around his wife. "If so, then it'll be a whole lot more peaceful around here, then, won't it?"

She stared at the pair, debating whether to admonish them for interfering, but even as the words teetered on her tongue, she knew this talk with Dalton was long overdue. She needed to understand what sparked that kiss between them. Why since she'd been back did it seem he worked overtime to avoid her?

"You remember how to get up there?"

"The old mine road. Yes, I was with Aunt Rebecca when we escorted the Billings EMTs up there after the bear attacked Rein, remember?"

A few moments later as she drove the narrow two-lane road leading to the cabin, she considered whether meeting up with a bear might be less hostile than an encounter with Dalton.

Chapter Six

DALTON REMINDED HIMSELF THAT HE did have peanut butter tucked away in the cabinet at the cabin. He'd spent the greater part of the day in a folding chair after digging a hole for his fishing rod in the dark, rich dirt. Between doxing and listening for woodland friends that might meander by, he found himself daydreaming of the recent kiss he'd shared with Angelique and the firestorm it raised inside him.

"Doesn't look like the fish are being cooperative today."

Jarred alert by the voice, his chair tipped sideways, his boot kicking the rod. At that moment, the line went taut. Sprawled on the ground, he army crawled, reaching for the pole as he watched the expensive rod skitter across the ground and disappear with his catch into the fast-moving river. With a sigh, he glanced over his shoulder, his eyes landing on a pair of slender legs encased in worn denim. A tease of tan skin peeked through a hole in one knee. He let his gaze travel upward and he saw a picnic basket. He caught a whiff of apple pie and his stomach growled plaintively. He'd not eaten lunch in anticipation of a healthy all-you-can-eat fish fry.

"Sorry about the rod. Didn't mean to startle you."

He pushed to his knees, righted his chair, with a definitive thud and, with another sigh, stood to face his current frustration—in more ways than one. "What are you doing here?" he muttered, not in the mood for company, least of all *this* woman.

"Saving you from starvation, it appears."

Not favoring the jab with a response, he folded his chair, grabbed his cooler and tackle box, and started back to the cabin. "You came all this way to bring me supper?" He wasn't being gracious. Wasn't in the mood. She'd just cost him a brand new rod and reel, not to mention a week of sleepless nights. But he wasn't about to let her know that. He swung around to face her, glad when she stopped in her tracks—those dark eyes waiting, watching him. She'd come from the BBQ, dressed in old jeans and a plaid snap-front plaid shirt. Her long, dark hair was pulled over one shoulder in a freeform braid. Her mouth-watering gaze held his in challenge and he battled between kissing her senseless or turning her over his knee for interrupting his solitude. Either way, he grew hard, adding to his frustration. He let the cooler hide his body's reaction. Shaking his head, he turned on his heel, making a beeline for the cabin, hoping she'd climb back in her truck and leave before things got complicated. He heard the crunch of pine needles as she followed him, right up the steps of the front porch. Without preamble, he faced her and plucked the basket from her hands. "Tell Rebecca thank you, as I suspect she's the one who put this together."

"And me? I brought the damn thing to you." She planted her fists on her hips.

He studied her. "Your thoughtfulness is appreciated. If you leave now, you'll just about make it back to town before dark. That road gets dicey after the sun goes down."

She didn't budge. Dammit.

"I figured it was time we hash out this thing between us."

"Thing? What thing?" He dropped the basket by the screen door and folded his arms over his chest in an attempt to look intimidating. Though he doubted it would work, at least it kept him from touching her.

One brow dropped as she eyed him. "You mean to stand there and tell me that you haven't given one second of thought to what happened behind the barn?"

Oh, hell yeah, he'd given it plenty of thought, reliving it only about a million times, his brain (and other parts) taking the fantasy to the next step. "It was just a kiss. We've been down that road. And if memory serves, you made it clear that it wouldn't happen again."

She licked her lips and looked away. He should have, too, but his eyes were caught on her mouth. She angled him a look. "We need to find a way to diffuse the tension between us. It appears to be causing a ruckus at the ranch." She rolled her eyes in disbelief. "My family feels it's creating bad karma, and honestly, can you blame them with all that's happened?"

He had a good idea of what would help ease tensions, but he was pretty sure she'd not agree to the suggestion. A deep roll of thunder caused him to look up in the dusky shadows of the afternoon, realizing that the storm threat grew nigh. "Looks like you're cooking dinner, then."

"I need to roll up my windows." She started down the steps and he stopped her, trotting down past her.

"Go on inside, I'll get them. Anything else you need?"

"Just my backpack."

He shook his head. Most women he knew carried some kind of fancy name-brand purse. Not this woman. Fat rain drops splattered on the ground, and in the next breath he was caught in a frog-strangling downpour. Hurrying back, he ducked through the screen door that Angelique held open for him. "Your pack." Dangling on the end of his finger, he held it out to her.

"You're soaked." She took the bag. "Thanks."

He glanced at the small round table with its four mismatched chairs. She'd set out paper plates, picnic utensils, and had a spread of food that made his mouth water. "I just need to change this shirt," he said, peeling off the sodden garment without thinking. He heard a soft gasp.

"I'll start a pot of coffee on the stove," she offered.

"The pot is in the cabinet above the stove. Coffee is in the cooler." Jed loved the old percolator pots. Not particular in many things, coffee—good coffee—was crucial to his step-dad. When he built the cabin, one of the first things he did was make sure they had a small cook stove with a burner hot enough to brew a pot of coffee. Dalton had acquired the taste at an early age, and tonight he was going to need it.

He grabbed a towel from the box of supplies and dried off. His jeans were a little wet, but tolerable. He was grateful, given how his dick strained against his zipper. Dalton caught her hooded glances as she measured out scoops of coffee. There was no question of the attraction between them. Sexual tension crackled as strong as the storm outside. They both felt it and played at ignoring it. But it had been simmering ever since that night of the reunion. Despite the heat, Dalton was faced with the cold reality that she wasn't interested in a guy like him—not for the long haul, anyway. He was a dark horse, scarred, and she'd let him know more than once how she felt about his drinking. She deserved better.

The storm had ushered in a cold front, causing a wind to circle like a spirit through the front screen and open windows. Angelique dove for the napkins and paper plates before the ornery breeze could snatch them and toss them to the floor. "Maybe we should close the door."

Dalton nodded and paused as he eased the door shut. Out of habit, he reached up shoved the latch into place. He met her wide-eyed gaze as he turned to face her. "Relax. I'm not going to try anything." He tossed it out as a joke, but it served as a reminder to himself. "It's a little chilly, do you mind if I start up the fire?"

She shrugged. "Sure," she said. In less time than it took him to find matches, she'd pulled a hoodie from her backpack and zipped it up to her neck.

Point taken, he knelt and assembled a fire. He wondered if she'd assessed that beyond the kitchen, the only furniture in the one-room cabin was a set of bunk beds in the corner, a rocking chair, and a sleeper sofa that might have seen better days. Jed preferred to keep things simple, uncluttered. Likely no woman had ever set foot in this place before now. He couldn't remember at any time Jed and his mom sneaking off into the wild. The woods weren't her thing, which often made him wonder how she wound up with Jed, a self-made man with a generous spirit who desperately wanted a family of his own. It didn't take Dalton long to realize that Eloise had been shopping for a man like Jed all her life, someone she could entrust to raise her boys so she'd be free to run away and find herself.

They ate dinner, mostly in silence with the occasional comment on how badly the area needed the rain. He lit every oil lamp in the place. The dim light only enhanced her beauty.

"We could try to be friends," she suggested, looking at him across the table. Those dark eyes sparkled. She lifted her shoulder as she took a sip from a tin mug she found in the basket. "Sally and Rein found a way to be friends."

Dalton held his tongue, stuffing food in his mouth to refrain from reminding her that Rein and Sally hadn't experienced steamy sex in the cab of a truck during a fierce storm…much like this one. *Shit.* He shifted uncomfortably, scowling at himself for his lack of control.

"Okay." She set her cup down and leaned her elbows on the table. "I'll start." She let out a small sigh. "Everyone around here has been very welcoming. Aimee graciously included me in her wedding, Wyatt agrees that I should come out to help Uncle Mike on weekends, even Clay Saunders—who I met for maybe two seconds before I left today—showed me more kindness than you've shown to me the entire time I've been back."

Dalton chewed his food, perhaps more slowly than normal as he listened, debating how to respond. "I thought Clay was depressed, unsociable." He looked up and met her stupefied gaze.

"That's what you got from everything I said? Nothing else?"

"Well, there is something I've been curious about, but I don't suppose it's really any of my business."

She raised one perfect brow. "You're probably right, but if will help clear the air, then bring it." She wiggled her fingers at him.

He dropped his fork on the empty plate and sat back. Crossing his arms, he eyed her. "You want me to be honest, right? Get it all out on the table?"

She held his gaze, worrying the corner of her lip. He fairly saw the wheels turning, the debate going on inside her as to whether or not she wanted to hear what he had to say. Finally, she nodded.

"Your husband is killed in Afghanistan, and soon after your daughter is living with her aunt and uncle here, while you're still in Chicago. Why is that, Angelique? What kind of mother just up and pawns off her kid for someone else to raise?" He saw the stab of hurt flicker in her eyes.

"You're right. It's none of your business. But I had my reasons, and they were what I felt was best for my daughter at the time." She tipped her head and narrowed her eyes. "But who are we really talking about here, Dalton? Me, or your mother?"

He snorted. "Just curious, I guess. Maybe I just won-

dered if you could shed some light on it from the perspective of a mother."

Her gaze was icy. "For starters, I'm not your mother
and my circumstances were nothing like hers." She rose
and began collecting the plates, stuffing them in the trash.

Maybe he was looking for an excuse to push her away.
Maybe when he looked at her, it reminded him of what
he'd suffered when his mom ran off leaving them with
Jed. "Look, I didn't intend for this to get ugly." He stood,
trying to help clear the table, succeeding only in having
his hand batted away.

She pointed a plastic fork covered in potato salad at
him, shaking it in his face. "You all but accuse me of
abandoning my child and dare to equate me to your
mother and whatever her reasons were, and I'm not supposed to take offense to that?"

He wiped a stray blob of salad from his shirt. "Look,
you're right." He felt like shit, but it didn't quell his curiosity. "I don't know what *your* reasons were."

Slamming the lid on the basket, she scooped it over
her arm and grabbed her backpack on the way to the
door.

"You can't go out there in this crap. The roads are
pure mud by now."

She whirled to face him, her eyes blazing. "You're so
damn good at casting judgments, aren't you? But let anything invade your little world and you're off in a heartbeat, drowning your troubles away at Dusty's."

Her words hit hard, worse than a fist to his gut. He
deserved it. "I know. You're right. It's what I do, how I
cope, it has been for years."

Her anger softened, replaced by confusion.

"Rein, Wyatt, hell, even Dusty have been after me for
a while now about my drinking. I'm working on it. Just
not as fast as everyone would like." He blew out a breath.

This was going to be the longest damn night of his life. "Look, you're going to have to stay until morning. I'd be in one hell of a mess with everyone if anything happened to you."

Studying him a moment longer, she relinquished the basket to him. He sat it on the table and raked a hand over his head. Now what? He glanced at her. "You want to tell me what happened in Chicago?"

She walked over and sat on the couch, letting her backpack fall to her feet. "Not yet. I'm just not ready, Dalton. But I swear to you, had I felt there was another choice, I'd never have left my daughter. She was safest with my aunt and uncle. Growing up, they were the closest thing to parents I had. That's why Emilee calls them her grandparents and I'm okay with that, as are they. I spent more time at their house than I did mine."

This was new to him—then again, how much had he tried to get to know her back then? She was a gawky middle school kid. He was a struggling teen, trying to find his identity, to make a name for himself, portraying himself as the town badass. Hell, even that night at Dusty's it'd taken Sally to point out his idiocy.

Dalton purposely sat on the opposite end of the room, guilt plaguing him for wanting to hold her and kiss away the sadness on her face. He thought back to that night. Dropping her off, driving home in a daze. Stunned not by what had happened, but at the powerful effect it'd had on him. By the time he figured things out, she'd returned to Chicago and soon after he'd heard she'd gotten married.

The realization that he'd been her one last fling came like a sucker punch to his gut. He'd always been the one in control of his affairs, calling the shots, causing the heartbreak. It was a blow to his pride. That's how he chose to look at it in the final analysis. Had she broken his heart? Was that what all this was about? Jesus. He fervently wished there was a Scrabble board, Chinese checkers, even a damn deck of cards in this cabin.

"I'm sorry, Dalton. What happened was my fault. I coerced you, and it wasn't fair."

He stared into the fire, choosing his words carefully. "I don't remember being an unwilling participant, Angel."

"So, it meant nothing."

His gaze snapped to hers. "I didn't say that."

"If it did then why didn't you say something? Why did you just let me go?"

He dropped to his knee, busied himself with poking at the fire as he searched for an answer that made any sense. "You were headed back to your life in Chicago." He glanced over his shoulder.

"Maybe you didn't want to be tied down," she offered.

He stood and looked at her. "Maybe that's true, but I'm not the man I was back then."

She held his gaze. "No, I don't think you are. I'm not the same either. I've been through some things, Dalton. I've made some poor choices. I'm in no position to pronounce judgments on anyone. I'm sorry for what I said about your drinking." She held her hands clasped in her lap.

An old transistor radio sat on the cabinet in the kitchen. It was used mainly for weather, and he wasn't even sure if the batteries inside still worked. He went over and turned it on, grimacing at the amount of static he found as he turned the dial. Then Garth Brooks filled the silence in the room with a song about a man who'd do anything for the woman he loved. *"I'm shameless."*

He shoved the coffee table aside and held out his hand to her. "You've got to get past this idea of being afraid of me, Angel."

Her reach hesitated midway to his. "I'm not—"

He grabbed her hand and gently brought her to her feet. They stood toe-to-toe as he watched her eyes slowly lift to his. "I'm not going to hurt you. But you need to know that ever since you've been back, I've been fighting my attraction to you. Something happened that night. I'm no saint, and I don't pretend to be one. I think you already know that."

"I've heard you have a reputation," she offered with a hint of a smile.

She allowed him to draw her closer, to circle his arm around her waist as they began to move to the music. "No one has plagued my sleep like you have." It felt good to admit it, to get it out in the open. Where it would take them, he didn't know, didn't care. Right now, he was content to have her snuggled up warm against him, dancing slow on the old braided rug. His body heated at her touch and he pulled her closer.

She looked up at him. "Did you mean what you said about plaguing your sleep?"

He cupped her face and smiled, realizing how his hands trembled. Gliding his thumb over her bottom lip, he imagined how she'd taste, the need in her kisses, the need that had been building inside of him since she arrived. He searched her eyes. "I meant every word. But if you don't feel the same, if you aren't ready for this, you need to stop me right now."

"I have a confession to make." She watched his mouth close in, his eyes searching hers.

"Yeah?"

"I haven't been sleeping well since that kiss behind the barn."

"It was pretty hot." His warm breath teased her lips, causing her to reach on her tiptoes to meet him. She clung to his shirtsleeves, taking as much as giving to a kiss that drugged her senses.

So much she wanted to tell him, needed to tell him, before they went any further. "Dalton," she sighed, tilting her head to accommodate his mouth blazing fire on her skin. His mouth expertly diverted her attention as he peeled the hoodie from her shoulders and unsnapped her shirt. Turning, he sat on the couch and pulled her to his lap, capturing her mouth in a searing kiss. When at last he let her come up for air, he held her gaze as he unhooked her bra, tossing it aside with her shirt.

Needing to feel his hard flesh to hers, she tugged off his shirt and reached for his waistband. With a wicked smile, he covered her hand with his.

"I want your nights to be as tormented as you've made mine." He held her gaze, releasing her face as he slowly slid his hands down over her breasts. Caressing, his mouth followed, sending heat to her core.

She arched against him an ache throbbing deep inside her.

"I want to see all of you, Angel," he whispered as he held her face from another mind-blowing kiss.

She stood and pulled him to his feet. With the steady thrum of the rain on the roof, they undressed each other between unhurried kisses.

"You're so beautiful," he said building a slow-burning need with his gentle caresses, his mouth that trailed fire over her body.

This patient side of him was unexpected. Angelique needed this, needed him. Overwhelmed by his tenderness, she surrendered to him, guiding him as he left a trail of fire down her body, between her thighs. The pure intimacy of the moment caused a gasp to escape her lips. Tears pricked at the back of her eyes.

"Baby, what's wrong?" His voice was gentle, soothing. It had been forever since she felt so loved, protected.

"Just happy," she answered with a wobbly smile.

"Aw, sweetheart." He leaned down brushing his lips to hers, and pushed into her igniting the fire that had been building between them. She met each thrust, her gaze locked with his as they drove each other. She had no delusions, willing to accept whatever he gave her. Her body shattered and she clung to him, her arms wrapped tightly around him as his body shuddered, and he followed her over on his own release.

He kissed her gently. "I'll be right back."

Angelique took a cleansing breath, and laying a hand over her heart, used the other to draw a quilt over her nakedness. Her body sated, she tempered her joy with caution, reminding herself that sex with Dalton was amazing, but that so much more was at stake. She couldn't afford the emotional toll of sacrificing her heart to someone who needed saving, who would take her trust, her heart, and toss it away when they were done. Though she felt a measure of guilt in her cynical view, it was trust—in him and in her emotions—that prevented her from telling him the truth about Emilee.

A few moments later, he returned, crawled beneath the blanket, and drew to his side, draping his arm around her. Together, they sat in silence staring into the fire.

"I have a confession," he said, kissing her temple.

She looked up at his profile and wondered for an instant what it would be like to wake to that each morning. She snuggled closer, breathing in his warm scent, wishing this moment would go on forever. That the secrets, the lies of omission, didn't matter. That they could truly be happy like this.

"I saw you once way back in high school. I was driving that old truck that Jed made all of us share." He chuckled low. "I was late for doing chores and took the shortcut past your uncle's farm. You were flying across

the field riding some coal-black horse, as if you were being chased by demons. It stopped my heart, not kidding.
One of the most beautiful sights I'd ever seen. You didn't
see me, but I damn near put my truck in the ditch that
night watching you."

"Stop it." She nudged his arm.

"Damn impressive, I thought to myself. That was the
first time I think I noticed you."

"And here all this time I thought I was invisible to
you."

He smiled. "Hey, I was an upperclassman. Was I going
to admit that a girl I knew in middle school was *kind of*
cute?"

"*Kind of* cute?" she repeated sitting up straighter to
look him in the eye.

He lifted the quilt and offered her a wicked grin. "A
cute girl who grew up nicely, by the way, and in all the
right places, I might add."

She snatched the covering and raised her brow.

"Go ahead, it's your turn."

Angelique eyed him in surprise. "My turn? What do
you mean, my turn?"

"Come on, I heard that maybe you had a bit of a
crush on me back then."

She shrugged. "Oh, *that*. I guess I thought you were
kind of cute. But my Aunt Rebecca would have locked
me in my room if she thought anything would come of
it."

His smile dissolved. "What do you think she'd say
now?"

Angelique met his solemn gaze. This was no longer
a teenage crush. He just didn't know it yet. As much as
what they'd shared meant to her, the reality was that they
had only begun to get to know each other again. Still,
the look on his face made her realize the importance of

her response. She touched her hand to his cheek. "She believes you're a good man, a hard worker, and that you love your family very much." She repeated what her aunt had said about Dalton when she'd asked how Angelique felt about him.

As though reading her mind, he held her gaze. "And what do you see?"

She searched his eyes, absentmindedly chewing the corner of her lip.

He brushed an errant wisp of hair from her eyes. "You do that when you're nervous."

"I'm not nervous."

"I put you on the spot. You don't have to answer."

"No, it's not that." She put her hand on his arm. "I'm not sure you're ready for what I have to say."

He straightened slightly as though preparing for the worst. An unwelcome chill separated them. "Go on. Whatever you have to say, just say it." The guard he used to keep pain at bay went up.

"Dalton, please. It's nothing bad. I just don't know how you'll react."

The coldness in his expression softened. "Try me."

She was attracted to him. Clearly, they had the physical thing down, but could she trust him with her heart?

"Angel?" He held her chin, forcing her eyes to his. "Do you want me to tell you what I see?"

She nodded. "You know, you're the one only who's ever called me that." Her smile wobbled.

He shifted, framing her face with his hands. "I see a beautiful, vibrant woman whose success has come from a lot of hard work and, I suspect, a lot of heartache. I'm not looking to hurt you, Angel. I want this—whatever it is—to work out between us."

A tear slipped down her cheek. Dalton brushed it away with this thumb followed by a chaste kiss.

She covered his hand. "Dalton," she said quietly, even as he continued to place soft kisses on her eyes, her nose, her lips. Her thoughts grew muddled, lost in his tenderness. How many times had she fantasized him like this? Even after their night together. Even when she believed that they had no future and she'd settled for Tony. Fear of what Tony put her through, of how he'd almost killed her and Emilee surfaced, and she began to tremble. "Hold me, please. Just…hold me."

"Sssshh, it's okay, Angel." He stretched out on the couch, pulling her to his side. "I can do that." Tucking her under his arm, he brushed her shoulder as he cradled her body to his. She rested her cheek on his chest, comforted by the steady beat of his heart. "Just rest, sweetheart. Whatever you need, I'm here."

Residual fear gave way to fatigue and as her eyes drifted shut, Dalton's heartbeat and the rain on the roof melded as one.

∞

The lawyer for the defense was a sour-faced man. His beady grey eyes and thin-lipped mouth positioned themselves into a smirk as the jury foreman stood to read the verdict.

"On charges of secondary manslaughter, robbery, and kidnapping—guilty."

The judge gave a sentence of more than fifty years in the State Penitentiary. There'd been no appeal. Tony hadn't wanted one. He glanced over his shoulder as they led him away. His gaze found hers across the crowded courtroom and the corner of his lip curled in a sneer as if to say, "This isn't over yet."

"Angel, sweetheart, wake up. It's only a dream, honey. You were dreaming."

She sat up, confused at first. Wherever she was, it was pitch black except for the rays of a full moon shining a path of light across the dark room.

"Are you okay?"

A hand touched her arm and she nearly leapt from her skin.

"It's me, Dalton. Sweetheart, you're at my cabin, remember?"

Dragged from a deep sleep, she struggled to free herself over bare limbs and the confines of the quilt as her thoughts swirled. She needed to stand on her own two feet. "I'm...I'm okay." Her body was cold, and she felt clammy. Her heart still raced with the thunder of wild horses.

"You're safe, Angel."

She saw him in the shadows moving to the kitchen where he relit one of the lamps. Her breathing steadier now, she recognized the symptoms of the panic attack. She'd not had one in several months. Remembering her dream, she snatched up her clothes and held them to cover her nakedness. "Did I say anything...in my sleep?"

He reached out, but didn't come closer. She couldn't blame him for being cautious. "Only mumbling. Do you remember anything?"

Too clearly. Even now, she remembered the murderous look in Tony's eyes. Only her aunt and uncle knew the truth. Everyone else, including Dalton, believed her husband was dead. To her, he was as good as dead the moment he tried to drive off with Emilee. She knew she'd have done whatever was necessary to protect her daughter—then and now. No one in Chicago with the exception of her lawyer knew where she'd gone. Not once in four years, since their divorce was final, had she heard from Tony.

"Angel?" Dalton's soothing voice penetrated the haze in her brain, alleviating some of her restlessness. She realized she was shivering.

"It was only a dream, darlin', and dreams can't hurt you." He wrapped his arms around her, her clothes still wadded in her arms. "A nice hot shower would do you a world of good, what do you say?"

The suggestion sounded heavenly—that, and a hot cup of chamomile tea. "Wait, you have hot running water?"

"Okay, it might be more on the tepid side. Rein rigged it up. Solar generated heat. Great little contraption when it works right." He turned her ahead of him and picked up a battery-operated lantern. "Rein didn't care to do much hunting after the bear attacked him, so he'd tinker around the cabin and came up with this."

The bathroom, lined with warm pine planking, was no bigger than a good-sized apartment pantry, but it had the necessities. The shower was an old-fashioned, built-for-one variety with a cloth curtain that offered privacy.

Dalton turned on the water, and handed her a towel and washcloth. "As much as I'd love to wash your back, it ain't gonna happen in there. Besides, I think you might need a cup of strong—"

"Chamomile tea?" she asked, laying her clothes on the vanity. She glanced at him as she stepped into the shower.

He made a face. "Uh, yeah, I'll see what I've got. You relax and enjoy—shampoos, soap—should all be there."

"Dalton?" She peeked around the curtain.

"Yeah?" He paused at the door and looked over his shoulder.

The water sluicing over her had eased one set of tensions, but letting her gaze drift over his bare, broad shoulders and finely-honed backside created yet another.

"Careful, sweetheart. You keep looking at me that way and I may be tempted to test the structural soundness of a one-person shower."

"I wanted to say thank you."

He studied her for a moment, then walked over, a man entirely comfortable in his own skin. He kissed her.

"You're welcome," he said, searching her eyes, and then kissed her again. "Tell me to leave," he said quietly.

"Leave?" she asked, amazed at how his simple kiss could addle her brain. "You should...leave, yes." She shut the curtain on him and held her breath until she heard the door shut. Only then did she allow her tears to flow.

Chapter Seven

"SO, I DON'T SUPPOSE YOU want to share what's going on between you and Angelique?" Rein continued to brush the horse he'd been grooming over the past hour.

Lost in his thoughts, Dalton had stayed busy with his chores, glad to have the silence, glad Michael Grey-feather hadn't shown up yet. Rein's question was one he'd been chewing on. Twice more before they left on Sunday they'd made love, once on a blanket with the morning mist rolling off the river. It made him hard just remembering her eyes holding his, rocking with him in perfect rhythm. Later, they'd eaten toast and had coffee on the porch and he'd hoped she'd open up and talk more about her dream, about her life in Chicago. But the simplest touch seemed to spark an insatiable fire be-tween them. The only thing they'd agreed on was that she wasn't ready yet to invest in a full-blown relationship. He hadn't given the notion much thought either, until this past weekend. Ironic that now when he was ready to consider giving up his bachelorhood, the one woman he wanted wasn't ready.

He blinked and realized he'd been leaning on the shovel, staring off into space. He glanced over and met Rein's questioning look. "Nope." He shrugged. "Noth-ing really to talk about." He went back to work, refusing to tell his brother that he and Angelique had shared off-the-charts hot sex and he still burned for her.

"Nope, there's nothing you *want* to discuss, or nope,

nothing happened?" Rein sat down and proceeded to clean the brushes he'd used.

"Nope as in it's none of your business, or anyone else's for that matter." Dalton hung the shovel up on the wall next to Rein. He felt his brother's curious gaze.

"Interesting," Rein commented.

"Shit," he muttered, and faced Rein. "What does that mean?"

He shrugged. "Sounds like maybe things are going good between the two of you and you don't want to talk about it. That's all."

Dalton shot his nosy brother a look. "Hey, I seem to remember being told to butt out along about the time you and Liberty were slinking around here."

"Hey, that's your sister." Rein pointed a finger at him.

"Half-sister and you're changing the subject."

Rein held up his hand. "Okay, okay. Truce. I won't ask again." He shook his head and went back to work.

A punch of guilt caused Dalton to sigh. He caught Rein's steady gaze. "Look, I honestly don't know myself. We didn't exactly talk out our ten-year plan."

Reins brows slipped beneath his hat. "That must have been some weekend."

Dalton plopped down on a bale of hay. He tore off his ball cap and scratched his head. "The woman is making me crazy." He shook his head and chanced a look at his brother. Rein offered him a sly grin.

"That's just in their DNA, bro, when you find the one woman who has the ability to do so. Hell, Liberty had me tied up most days— "

Dalton held up his hand. "*That* I don't need or want to hear."

"It's a metaphor, idiot. Even now, she can drive me nuts sometimes. Thing is, I know better now how to get even when she starts driving me crazy."

"Yeah, and I *really* don't need to hear any of that, thanks just the same." Dalton tossed a frown at Rein.

"Okay, what I'm saying—"

"Poorly," Dalton interjected.

"What I'm saying is if the woman didn't mean something to you, she wouldn't have the power to drive you crazy."

Oh, hell yeah, he'd figured that much out. "I haven't heard a peep from her in over a week. I thought, you know, give her some time." He pushed to his feet and paced in front of Rein.

"The woman does work in a vet clinic and is raising a little girl," Rein reminded him.

"Do *we* drive women crazy like that?" Dalton scowled.

The question seemed to puzzle Rein. "I can't see how that's possible, except maybe in bed."

"You are living the dream, you know that?" Dalton nodded.

"And he's lying through his teeth." Liberty sauntered in and handed Rein his wallet. "You left that on the kitchen table, Casanova, thought you might need it." She glanced at Dalton. "And the answer to your questions is, yes. Men can drive women bat-shit crazy." She tipped her gaze to Rein. "And not just in bed, darlin'. Guys can be just as hard to figure out as women."

"Really?" Rein pushed up the brim of his hat and looked at her. "Like what am I thinking, right now?"

"That you wish we were back home in bed."

"Hey," Dalton said with a wave. "Did you all forget I was here?" This little foreplay between the two of them was not making things any easier.

He'd spent the week taking an inordinate number of cold showers and purposely pushing himself around the ranch, even rebuilding an old John Deere tractor that'd been sitting in the shed for decades. Just to keep his mind off her. Nothing had helped.

"I assume the woman in question Angelique?"

Dalton's head snapped up. "Who told you?"

She snorted. "Really? Like no one at the barbecue noticed that only you two were missing?"

Actually, he'd thought with so many people around that maybe no one would've have noticed. Dalton blew out a sigh.

"Listen, are you feeling restless, big brother?" Liberty asked.

He held up his hand to stop her. "Yeah, and I don't think I want to get into this."

His sister planted her fists on her hips. "Advice from him but not from me?"

"I wasn't asking for anyone's advice." Dalton stood and planted his hat back on. "I'm going to take a ride. Is the bike gassed up?"

Rein nodded.

"Hey, wait a sec. Can I just add something here?" Liberty interjected.

Dalton's shoulders slumped. "Sure, fire away. Just don't tell me what I *should* be doing to get her attention."

"Oh," Liberty said with a shrug, "okay, then, never mind, darlin'." She turned on her heel and faced Rein. "Sally's bringing out a couple of kids this afternoon. Will the new horse be ready?"

Dalton shifted from one foot to the other, debating whether or not he needed or wanted Liberty's opinion. Maybe he was the crazy one. Okay, maybe it wouldn't kill him to hear what she had to say, being a woman and all. "Okay, say I wanted to, you know, get her attention. Angelique's been through a lot and I don't want to—"

"Scare her off? Let her know how you really feel?" She faced him with a soft smile.

"Yeah, I guess." This was new territory for him. Women as a whole, not so much, but developing a relationship with one? He was stumbling around in the dark. All he knew was that without her there was a void, and when he was with her, like this weekend, he didn't feel confused or out of place.

"Let me ask you this, are you sleeping?" Liberty asked.

"Barely." Dalton sighed and looked away. There was no use in fighting it. Seemed like half the town knew about the two of them, even though they'd decided they wanted to keep things simple, low-key for now.

"Restless, I think we've established. Are you eating?"

Dalton threw her an exasperated look. "Is there a point to this?"

Liberty folded her arms over her chest. He had to admit living the country life had transformed her from a guarded Vegas nightclub dancer with an attitude to a woman at ease in her husband's flannel shirts and a pair of torn-up jeans. Her hair she now wore long in cinnamon-colored braids. The only evidence of her former life was her tongue piercing and he'd never questioned why she still had it. The only thing that hadn't changed was her bossy attitude. And he kind of liked that about her.

"You're in love with her," she stated primly.

Love? Come on. True, she was kin and so he'd give her that. And she'd married his brother, okay, but how the hell could she make such a determination after only, what? A couple of random questions? He waved off the notion. "I think maybe you're getting ahead of things."

Liberty cocked her dark eyebrow—the universal unspoken language women have of stating they are right and you are an idiot.

Dalton's gaze swung to Rein, who stood, walked over, and draped his arm over her shoulder in alliance. He closed his eyes. "I'm thinking you're both full of shit, that

it's way too damn early for that…but let's say, for the sake
of my sanity, that *is* the case. If someone doesn't feel the
same, then isn't it better to wait until, you know, everyone's on the same page?"

"And if everyone followed that rule, waiting for the
other person to speak up first, where would we be?"

He hated like hell that what she said made sense. Giv-
en the assumption that the reason for how crappy he'd
been feeling had something to do with…he couldn't
bring himself to think that he could be in love.

"You think I should—assuming you might be right—
tell her?" Accepting the possibility made him oddly less
concerned about his mental state, at least. Course, if she
didn't feel the same, he'd maybe go with that idea he once
had of moving to Oregon, becoming a smokejumper. Far
cry from shoeing horses, but he and Hank had batted the
idea around a few times.

"I don't think you're going to know until someone
speaks up and tells the other person how they feel."

Dalton needed to chew on this. "Yeah, maybe. I need
to clear my head. You guys okay if I take off for a couple
of hours?"

Rein waved him off. "Liberty will help me."

Hell, yeah, like the two of them would get anything
done. Liberty had given Rein the green light to start a
family and, well, suffice it to say no place was sacred if the
mood was right.

Dalton raised a hand, leaving the two behind, needing
to ride—to not think about Angelique or love or how
amazing her skin smells. He shaded his eyes to the morning sun. A good day to get lost on the mountain curves,
maybe take a dip in a cold mountain lake…which mys-
tified him when, twenty minutes later, he found himself
pulling into the Greyfeather's gravel drive.

∽∞∽

Angelique heard the rumble of the Harley cycle and knew immediately who it was. She'd tried all week to let what happened at the cabin stay at the cabin, putting all her energies into work at the clinic, helping her aunt bake and freeze pies ahead for the fall festival in town. She'd taken evening rides with Emilee, soaked in long, luxurious bubble baths, but nothing had worked to keep him from causing her sleepless nights thinking of how it'd been between them. He'd been as open with her as Dalton could be, but neither had spoken of or promised anything beyond the idyllic weekend they'd spent in total privacy.

A knock rattled the old screen door and she moved from the living room into the foyer. Her heart stopped as she spotted him standing there in faded jeans and scuffed boots, his black t-shirt molding to his muscled body. She noticed from his profile that he'd not bothered to shave yet. He turned then and looked at her, his gaze unreadable in his dark sunglasses. The man should have a warning label stamped on his forehead.

"Good morning." He tore off his glasses and those dark amber eyes held hers. He hooked his thumb in his jeans pocket. "Is Emilee around?"

Her heart, already on a slippery slope, skittered to a stop. She took a steadying breath and licked her lips before answering. His gaze dropped to her mouth. She rested her hand on the door to steady herself. "She went to Billings this afternoon with her grandparents."

His head snapped up, his eyes flashing with an awareness that caused her fingers to ball into a fist. "Beautiful morning for a ride. May I ask what you wanted to see Emilee about?"

He looked away and she held her breath. A million explanations paraded through her head—how she hadn't known for sure the baby was his, how she'd been afraid that she'd ruin his life, that he'd had enough on his plate back then. None of them sounded worthy of forgiveness.

He sighed. "To be honest, I came to see you."

"Oh?" she managed to squeak out.

"I wondered if maybe you'd like to go for a ride?"

She twisted the old hook dangling from the door-frame. "I don't know if that's such a good idea."

He looked down at his boots and nodded. "Because you're not interested?" He glanced at her, narrowing one eye with a quizzical look.

She drew her teeth over her bottom lip, forcing her-self to stop when she noticed the corner of his mouth lift in a knowing grin. "If you must know, it's that I am interested, not that I'm not...interested."

He scratched his brow and walked to the edge of the porch. He stood searching the horizon before turning on his heel and, in two strides, putting his face up to hers with nothing but the screen between them. "Maybe we should try something normal."

"Normal?" She wanted nothing more than to pull him through that screen and have her wicked way with him—or vice-versa. *Stop*, she mentally chided herself. Her resolve grew weaker each moment she stared into his handsome face.

"Normal, meaning go for a ride. Stop someplace, maybe get a bite to eat. Talk about this" —he gestured from him to her— "about us."

"There is no *us*, Dalton."

He shook his head. "Yeah, well I'm not making that same mistake twice." He looked away, then challenged her with a steely look. "Unless you tell me right now you don't feel a damn thing for me. Then, I swear to God, I'll leave you alone."

"Dalton."

"Look, Angel. I don't know everything, and that gives

you the advantage. You know it's a small town, you hear things, rumors—God knows I've been the flavor of the month from time to time." He paused and released a sigh. "I heard that your marriage wasn't the best, that you had your troubles."

He was trying to be polite. This was what she hated most about small towns. Gossip, rumors, hearsay—everyone always feeling the need to add in their two cents, poking their noses into other people's lives. She drew back her shoulders. "That is my business." She was ready to shut the door. Just walk away. God knows she didn't need to invite more drama into her life. And what would he do, how would he feel if he knew she'd lied by omission—not telling him about Emilee or that her ex-husband wasn't dead but very much alive in an Illinois prison? It was for his own good to let things end now, before things got more complicated. "I can't."

He studied her face, blinking as though absorbing what she'd said or deciphering what she hadn't. "Okay." He nodded. "Okay," he repeated, more softly. "I'll see you around."

He walked slowly down the steps—head up, those broad shoulders straight—and never looked back. She'd hurt him and his pride. Probably lost her last chance at something she'd search for the rest of her life.

"Dalton?" His name came out before she realized it. He glanced back at her.

"Give me a minute." She jotted a quick note and left it on the kitchen table, then pulled on her cowboy boots and grabbed her hoodie before slipping her purse over her body. Checking her phone battery, she closed the front door and found him seated on the bike, holding out a helmet to her. "You just happen to have an extra helmet?"

The grin he gave her nearly turned her bones to liquid. "I took a chance."

"Where are we going?" she asked as she settled in behind him.

"Guess we'll know when we get there." He started the bike, its motor roaring to life. "Hang on tight," he called over his shoulder.

She clamped her arms around him, snuggling close. "Like this?" she asked over his shoulder.

He grinned. "Just like that, darlin'."

He took the curves with breathtaking speed, so much so that a time or two she buried her face in his shirt, squeezing her eyes until they reached a straight stretch of road. Once she got used to the nuances of balance and speed, she relaxed more. Comforted by the warmth of his back pressed to her body, she took in the beauty of the back roads he'd found, zipping through little wide spots in the road that she didn't know existed in the mountains. Sometime later, he pulled into a diner at the edge of an old mining town, still trying to hang on with one or two tourist stops. They ate buffalo burgers at one of the sagging picnic tables on a scenic overlook behind the diner.

"Are you having fun?" he asked, watching her over his frosty root beer.

She hadn't felt this free in such a long time. Well, not since their time at the cabin. She nodded. "It's not quite as scary as it looks."

"You want to learn to drive? I can teach you."

She choked on her drink. "Uh, no, I think it might be wise to get a little more practice as a passenger first."

"Oh, come on, this from a woman who rides wild horses like you do?"

She smiled and ducked her head. "Maybe someday." She looked up at him. "Yeah, this has really been fun." Being with him, teasing each other, enjoying a beautiful day…it was more than she could ever imagine.

"So, kind of a funny story," he said, removing his glasses to rub his eye.

She waited, smiling at how open he seemed, how at ease. This wasn't the brooding, angry man she'd been used to seeing. He seemed genuinely…happy.

"So, I'm talking to Rein and Liberty, who I think likes having a brother she can bounce her bossy ass opinions on. Anyway, she makes this suggestion." He glanced away, looking out over the tops of the pines in the valley below.

She waited and then chuckled. "Okay, I'll bite. What was her suggestion?"

He searched her eyes before continuing. Whatever it was, she could see him stalling. "Yeah. You don't know this, but I used to have this dream about being a smoke-jumper. They've got schools out in Oregon—that's where I thought I'd go."

Fear that he was gearing up to tell her he planned to leave settled cold in her stomach. She swallowed hard and laid the rest of her food on her plate. "You're moving to Oregon? You haul me clear out here in the middle of nowhere to tell me that?" She started up from the table and he grabbed her hand.

"No, I'm not, but I'm curious, would that bother you?"

She pressed her palm to her forehead, letting his question settle in her jumbled brain. Hell, yeah, it would bother her. But she wouldn't be the one to stop him from doing what he wanted to do. "Look, did Liberty suggest you move? Because, you know, I bet they have schools right here. I mean, look around you, nothing but trees for miles."

His mouth crooked in a smile. "No, Liberty didn't suggest anything of the sort. Why would you think that?"

She stared at him, lifting her arms to her sides. "Because you said that Liberty had suggested something to you."

"Oh, right." He tugged her back to her seat. "Sit down, I'm getting to that."

Rattled, she took a calming breath as she settled across from him. "Ok, so you've thought about becoming a smoke jumper." She wanted to ask him why he'd choose such a dangerous profession, but she feared she might never hear Liberty's suggestion. "If you could just get to Liberty's suggestion?"

He swallowed hard and nodded. He looked visibly nervous, this guy who was afraid of nothing.

"Okay, she said that one of us had to speak up, or, you know, the human race as we know it might end."

"Are you feeling well?" She studied his face. At this point, she had to wonder how he'd become the communications end of the ranch business ventures. "You do know you aren't making a lick of sense?"

He shook his head. "I have feelings for you, Angel."

The fear returned—not as before, but in a way that made her unsure she'd heard him correctly. That her mind was merely playing tricks on her. She wasn't sure how or if she should respond.

"Ideally, this is where you tell me that you have similar feelings…for me. If, in fact, that is the case."

He hadn't let go of her hand, she realized. This was not like him at all. And while she wanted to play along, part of her had trouble accepting what she heard. "Dalton, I couldn't have—wouldn't have had spent the weekend with you had I not had feelings for you."

He nodded, seeming to accept that reason. "So, a couple of questions—if you don't mind?"

She shrugged. "Shoot."

"Have you slept well this week?"

"Barely." She liked the feel of her hand wrapped in

the warmth of his.

"Eaten much?"

She frowned and looked down at her half-eaten meal, realizing it was the most she'd eaten all week. "Not really, my stomach has felt strange."

"Right! It was the same for me. Restless. Not sleeping, not eating. I thought I was losing my mind."

She wanted to empathize, but it was clear those same things occurred after Emilee was born, so it wasn't as alarming as it seemed for him. "Okay?"

He chuckled, but his eyes were locked to hers. "Liberty suggested that maybe I was in love. Me? Can you believe that?"

She shrugged. "What's so hard to believe? You deserve to be happy as anyone else, right?"

He frowned and she willed him to just come out and say it—say the words she'd dreamt forever of him saying to her. "So, who's the lucky girl?" she prodded him.

He blinked. "You, of course. I honestly tried to fight it." His gaze shot to hers. "No offense."

"None taken," she answered quietly. Her heart pounded against her ribs. She was not about to cry and spoil this moment.

"The more I thought about what she said, the more it made sense."

"Makes sense," she uttered, her words barely a whisper. How many times had she played this moment out in her fantasies? Sitting atop a rundown mountainside diner at a dilapidated picnic table was *not* one of the scenarios she'd imagined, but it would do just fine.

"So, there it is."

Her cell phone jangled and she smiled, seeing that it was her aunt. "Excuse me, it's Aunt Rebecca. Do you mind?" She hated to ruin the moment, but her mom radar went on full alert. "Everything okay?"

"We're having a wonderful time. I wondered if you'd mind if we took Emilee to the American Indian Museum and then I might have promised her a new outfit for the first day of school. After that, I thought maybe we'd eat dinner here. That is, if you're not too lonely at home without us."

She looked up at met Dalton's steady gaze. "I'm actually out."

"Oh, I forgot Sally was taking some kids from the Billings teen home to the ranch today. Did she need some help?"

"Um, I'm not with Sally." Dalton had cleaned up the table and sat on his bike, waiting on her. "Dalton came by and took me on a motorcycle ride."

"Ah, that's nice, dear. You two must have found a way to get along."

"You could say that. It's been a long week."

"And I bet you haven't told him yet the real reason why you came to the cabin last weekend."

"How'd you—"

"Sweetheart, where do you think Emilee gets her gift of sight?"

Angelique glanced at Dalton. He'd just laid his heart out to her—how could she tell him and risk destroying that trust? "I don't know what to say to him."

"The truth is always a good place to start."

She walked away, putting a little distance between them to make sure she was out of earshot. "I don't want to end this before it even gets off the ground." She sighed. "He told me he's in love."

"With you?"

"Yes. I mean, he didn't come right out and say those words. It was Liberty who suggested the idea because he wasn't eating or sleeping…"

"So now he thinks he's in love."

"That's about the size of it, yes."

"And what about you? Are you in love with him?"

Angelique considered the thought. "I've loved him for as long as I can remember. I'm not sure I ever thought he'd ever have feelings for me."

"Maybe you should accept it and see where it takes you?"

"I'm scared. There it is honestly, Aunt Rebecca." She'd realized her greatest fear. If she let herself love him, would he understand? Would he accept the secrets she'd kept from everyone, but especially from him? "I don't want to lose him."

"My dear, you have to believe that a love that is meant to be is able to find a way through even the most difficult times. You need to find out how true this love of yours is. Don't worry about Emilee. We'll see to her. She'll probably fall asleep in the car.

"Thank you, Aunt Rebecca. I may see you anyway at home."

"We'll see," she answered. "Go on, now. I imagine he's been patiently waiting."

"He has." They said their goodbyes and she tucked her phone in her purse.

He slid his glasses on as she walked toward him. He handed her a helmet. "Everything okay?"

"Oh, sure, they just want to show Emilee the museum, buy her clothes, spoil her rotten." She climbed up and wrapped her arms around him.

"That's kind of what grandparents are supposed to do, right? You should see Aimee's mom around Gracie June." He shook his head and chuckled, then looked over his shoulder. "Guess that leaves you alone tonight for supper, huh?"

"Yeah, I guess it does."

"I'd be happy to cook you supper at my place," he

said.

Angelique considered her aunt's advice. "I'd like that."
She leaned her chin on his shoulder.

"And what if I offer desert first?" he said, his mouth
lifting in a wicked grin.

"I guess we'll know when we get there," she said, repeating his words. His laugh melded with the roar of the
bike as he kicked it to life.

Chapter Eight

THE SWEET SCENT OF HER curled against him awoke his senses, causing his body to stir. Dessert had come first. Barely able to make it inside the cabin, they'd left a path of clothing from the front door to the bedroom. He'd been grateful that, when they'd arrived late afternoon, no one seemed to be around. He'd guessed they'd all gone up to see the progress on Rein's and Liberty's house up near the lake.

He let his eyes adjust to the deepening shadows. It was well after sunset, though he hadn't given much thought to the time. He shifted, drawing her closer, amazed by her silky skin, roused by every soft curve, by how she responded to his touch.

"You're insatiable," she said through sleep-induced huskiness.

It was true. Just a look from her these days could arouse him.

She turned in his arms and lay facing him. Her dark eyes shone in the dim light. "What time is it?" she asked, tracing his mouth with her fingertip.

"Past supper. You hungry?"

She smiled. "You did promise me food."

"You distracted me." He leaned in to kiss her soft mouth, unable to get enough. "See, there you go again." He eased her to her back.

She curled her hand in his hair, offering long, mind-numbing kisses. More than once they'd made love, lazily exploring, teasing, and satisfying each other. With each passing moment, he relinquished a bit more of his heart, his freedom to her. Warm and ready, she accepted him once more, moving slowly, relishing the union. Amid whispered sighs, she held him close, giving as much as she took, driving his need, pushing, challenging. She grabbed the pine rails of the headboard, eyes closed in bliss, lost to the passion incarnate between them. Her lips parted on a silent gasp and he captured her mouth, claiming her even as they surrendered to one another.

Rolling to his side, he realized that he'd let desire overrule his senses, forgetting protection. He drew her under his arm, part of him ready to welcome a child should one come of their union. Is this what it was to know when you'd found that one person? He covered her hand, resting on his heart. His body still thrummed, but the desire to tell her how he felt, the increasing need to know if she felt the same, made him nervous. *Ridiculously fucking nervous.* He chuckled at the notion. Every time they were together, he discovered something new about himself. "You keep distracting me, Angel, and we may never eat again." He placed a kiss on her forehead and took a cleansing breath to steady his runaway heart.

"Maybe I'll shower while you go fix us something to eat," she offered, and patted his chest.

Damn, he was beginning to unravel, the kind that gets you thinking about curtains and what color to paint the kitchen cabinets.

"And I'm supposed to be able to concentrate on food with that image in my brain?"

"You could try thinking of something else." She braced on her elbow and smiled down at him.

He probably could, but did he want to? Hell, no. At this moment, all was right in his world. Accepting that he loved this woman, surrendering his heart, his trust to her was the single, most peaceful certainty he'd had in his life. If she needed time to realize how good what they had between them was, he could give her that. But if she changed her mind, he'd planned to make damn sure she knew what she was missing. A splinter of a thought festered in his brain, prompting his next comment. "This has been a great day."

"Motorcycles and sex, you can hardly beat that combination."

She meant it in a teasing way, but he had this need to let her know that this had become more than sex for him. He touched her face. God, she was more beautiful than the last moment, if that were possible. "I've dated lots of women, Angel."

"That's a boost for my ego." She smiled.

"Could you...please just let me get through this?" he asked, clamping her lips together with his fingers.

She rolled her eyes and he replaced his fingers with a kiss.

"Are you trying to get out of fixing supper again?"

Judas Priest. As if this wasn't hard enough. Exasperated by the fact that he'd managed to work up enough intestinal fortitude to say he loved her while she kept batting away his attempts made him question whether this was the best time to bare it all.

Senseless thinking, given they had little else to hide from each other.

"Are you afraid to hear what I have to say?"

Her smile faded and she stood, drawing the sheet around her. She took a couple of steps toward the bathroom and faced him. "I'm not very good with promises, Dalton. Have I enjoyed every moment we've shared? With all of my heart. Do I hope there will be more? Of course. What more do you want from me?"

Dalton stared at her, hearing the very same words he probably had said in one form or another to the countless women he'd dated. Some had lasted a day or two, his longest a week. It was a slap in the face to his pride, but the shot to his heart hurt like hell. He wiped his hand over his mouth. Maybe she didn't feel he was capable of more than this. Good times, a couple of laughs, hot sex, then back to business for good ol' Dalton—End of the Line's good-timin' man.

Had she not heard a word he'd said? Hadn't he all but laid it out there that he had real feelings for her?

"Dalton?"

He blinked and looked up, realizing she stood in front of him. She reached out and touched his face. Her dark hair spilled over skin he knew was soft as silk.

"I *do* care about you. Believe me."

He wanted to, but he'd never been in this position. He'd always been the sorry-ass that gave the *he cared* speech. On top of everything else, guilt of how shallow he must've sounded assaulted him. He couldn't do anything about the past, but by God, he still had his pride. He took her hand, easing it away as he stood. Looking down into those soulful eyes it was hard to realize he'd been so far off base. Sex, he understood. Maybe that was his destiny. The consummate bachelor—no wife, no family, no legacy. It was a kick-in-the-gut reality check. "I'll go scramble you some eggs, then I best get you back home."

Later, scowling at the frying pan, Dalton's sour mood hadn't dissipated much. His cell phone rang and he answered it, forgetting to first reel in his frustration. "What."

"Dalton?"

It was Clay Saunders. Dalton had stopped by his cabin once or twice to catch up and knock back a couple of beers this past week. Except for obvious challenges, his college buddy seemed to have things pretty well in check. "Hey, I figured maybe you'd gone up to see Rein's place with the rest of the family."

"Yeah, they asked. But I wasn't really feeling up to it. I'm just trying to settle in, you know. I have to say, that fire pit addition is damn sweet."

"You're welcome." Dalton's mouth crooked in a smile. "I built one behind every cabin. That view of the mountains is amazing."

"It's nice. I'm still getting used to this kind of quiet, though."

Dalton nodded. "It takes bit, but you'll get used to it. What can I do for you?"

"Yeah, I have a favor to ask."

Dalton tuned into the shower still running. "Sure, what's up?"

"I wondered what you know about Sally."

"Sally Andersen? You met her at the barbecue, right?"

"Yeah, that's the thing. I was, well, let's just say I was pretty much a dick." He sighed. "It was a bad night. I probably should have just come straight to the cabin. I really wasn't sure if this was where I needed to be right now in my life, you know?"

"I hear that." Dalton sighed. Oregon had recently shot back up to his top ten places to visit. He plated the scrambled eggs, dropped a piece of bacon and a slice of toast beside it. He'd brewed a pot of coffee and had finished his first cup when he caught sight of Angelique walking across his bedroom wrapped in a towel. He nearly forgot he was on the phone. He forced his gaze away. "So, what's the favor?"

"I'd like to have her number. She was trying to talk to me about some therapy horse program and I shut her down pretty hard. That happens sometimes. PTSD, so they say. But I hate what I do and say. It's not the real me. I thought maybe I could at least call and apologize."

"Sally's good people, Clay," he offered as a gentle

warning.

"I get it, really, and I'd understand if you didn't want to give me her number. But I'm not some lunatic stalker, if you're concerned for her safety."

Dalton scratched his neck. "Not my concern." He just didn't want to see Sally hurt.

"In my defense, I was tired from the trip and was ushered into a whole backyard of total strangers, besides Hank and Rein. Heard you'd gone AWOL. It all just blindsided me and I feel bad it about it. So, there you go."

"I understand, bro. More than you realize. I've been around this bunch for years and I still get hives around those big community gatherings." Dalton fished an old address book from a drawer slated for miscellaneous things.

"Dalton, no disrespect, but you don't get it. I'd give my good arm for a case of hives. At least you know what you're battling. The dozens of docs I've seem all say the same thing—in time it'll get better. But they can't tell me what triggers my anxiety."

Immediate guilt washed over him. The man had been through hell and back. Dalton didn't have a clue. "Hey, buddy, I can't imagine what it must have been like over there, how hard it's been since you been home. But one thing you can count on around here is no judgment. And truth is, it doesn't take PTSD to act like a dick. Trust me, this I do know."

A low chuckle came across the line. "Thanks, buddy."

Dalton read off the number, finishing the conversation as Angelique emerged from the bedroom fresh and fully dressed. "I see you found your clothes. They were kind of" —he gestured with a sweep of his arm—"everywhere."

"Thank you. This looks fantastic. Did I smell coffee? It hit me when I came out of the shower—which, by the way, is amazing. It's like having your own spa, and that showerhead—like standing in a rainforest."

He shoved away the image of her naked body under a gentle waterfall, surrounded by a lush green tropical forest. "Here's your coffee. Cream or sugar?"

"No, black is fine, thanks."

He sat down across from her, wanting to put as much space between them as possible.

"Everything okay?" she asked, blissfully unaware of how she'd rejected his heart.

"Yeah, why?" He glanced up, avoiding eye contact, trying to dismiss his feelings as easily as she had.

She shrugged. "You were on the phone awhile, so I guess I just wondered. Making conversation."

It was all he could do not to lie and mention that it was just an old girlfriend passing through town. In the end, the truth was more mature. "Clay wanted Sally's phone number."

"Oh?" That got her attention. "They just met at the barbecue last weekend. He works fast."

"Yeah, I don't think it's like that. He mentioned that he acted like a di—his behavior wasn't what he'd have liked it to be. He just wants to apologize." Dalton dug into his meal.

"Well, you never know. Clay is a handsome guy. Sally's beautiful fun, single. Stranger things have happened."

This sure as hell wasn't a conversation he wanted to be having—especially now, especially with her. "So, you can see the possibility between them, but not us?"

She set her fork down. "I can't do this. Maybe you should take me home." She dug in her purse and pulled out her phone. "On second thought, I'll call Sally."

He pushed from his chair and snatched the phone from her. "I told you I'd take you home." He searched her eyes, wanting answers to the many questions buzzing in his brain.

"I'm sorry that you're angry," she said a few moments later as he drove the back road to her uncle's farm.

"I'm not angry." A lie. He kept his eyes on the road, already cursing his decision to see her earlier today. It seemed a lifetime ago, this notion that he was in love, and it had blinded him to the fact that for it to feel good, it needed to be reciprocated.

The house was dark and the truck was not in the drive. Dalton pulled in and put his truck in gear, but didn't shut off the ignition. If all she wanted was sex, then they'd had it. The whole thing stung, worse than it had years before. This time there wasn't another man, no reason other than choice that she'd not be able to return the same feelings he had for her.

"Do you want to come in? We could sit on the porch, if you like."

Perplexed, he shifted in his seat and looked at her. "Now you want to be just friends—or wait, friends with benefits, right? At least this is what I'm reading here." He glanced away, his frustration growing by the second. This was damn sure a far cry from the thought he'd had four hours ago of Rein designing the perfect house. He'd never been so blindsided by a woman—with the possible exception of dear mom. She'd used Jed for what she needed, and then was gone when something better came along. Maybe he should be grateful things hadn't gotten that far with Angelique. Maybe her rejection was actually a point in his favor.

"It's more than that, Dalton. You know it is." She unbuckled to face him

"No, I don't. I know I was being honest with you, Angel. Maybe Liberty was wrong." He shook his head. This was as good a campaign for bachelorhood as anything. You put your trust in someone, chances are they're going to stomp on your heart.

"What Liberty said—"

"Was wrong," he slung back. "She doesn't know shit about me. She doesn't know you. How could she possibly think that anything would be different? That you're different from the dozens of other women I've known." The muscle in his jaw ticked as he looked out the window. He wanted answers. He wanted a stiff drink. He wanted her.

"I do care about you. There's more to this."

"Yeah?" He pinned her with a narrowed gaze. "Tell me, what is it that I'm not getting here, Angel? Is it another guy?"

She shook her head. "No."

"My drinking? Is that the issue?"

She folded her arms protectively over her chest and looked away from him. "It concerns me, I won't deny that, but it has nothing to do with my choices." She glanced at him, and he could see she was fighting back tears.

His frustration, the hurt, showed no mercy. "Then what? If it's my reputation, I swear there is no one in my life, Angel. No one I'd rather be with than you."

She shook her head and refused to look at him. He wanted to shake her, to make her see what she was tossing away. God, he was dying inside. He closed his eyes and took a deep breath before he looked at her. His heart twisted in his chest at what he was about to say. "Look, if you aren't interested in more than some good times with a guy like me, then hell, just come right out and say it. Because I can't take this. You won't talk to me. I can't help. I don't know what else to do, except let go."

She raised her eyes to his, tears streaming down her cheeks. "I didn't want this. I didn't mean for this to happen. I knew someone would get hurt. Why couldn't you leave things the way they were? Why didn't I?" She jerked the door open and he lunged for her arm.

"What are you talking about?"

She slid from the seat and out of his grasp. "Just please leave me alone. Leave Emilee alone. Please."

"Angel? What the hell? Just tell me what I've done."

"It's not you, Dalton. All this time, I've been living a lie. I've lied to you, to my daughter, and worse, I've lied to myself, thinking it wouldn't matter."

"You're not making any sense." He shut off the truck.

"No, please, you have to leave. Just go," she said, her sobs choking out the words.

"I can't leave you this way," he pleaded, not even understanding what the hell he was fighting for.

"I don't want to see you again, Dalton. Trust me, you're better off." With that, she slammed the door and tore up the steps, leaving him battered, bruised, and stunned.

Angelique hadn't heard from him in days. School was just around the corner and Emilee's excitement to see her friends and head into third grade had kept her busy. Whenever the opportunity to help her uncle at the Kinnison ranch came up, she used work as an excuse.

"You never mentioned how things are between you and Dalton," her aunt asked. They'd spent the afternoon cutting out a number of skirts from material they'd found at one of her aunt's favorite fabric shops. "We must have looked at five stores in Billings, searching for school clothes. Aside from the cost, the workmanship was ghastly. It's awful to think of what the mark-up must be." She spoke with a straight pin clenched in her teeth. "All it takes is a little time and the right machine."

Angelique smiled, remembering the number of times when she'd needed a special outfit for school. All she had to do was pick out a picture and magically, it seemed, her aunt found the same fabric and the right pattern to fit Angelique perfectly. She flipped the page of the book she'd been reading, wishing all her needs and wants could be so easily crafted. "Dalton and I have decided to be friends." A long silence followed, prompting her to look up from her book. She met Aunt Rebecca's steady gaze.

"Friends?" she repeated as though not hearing it the first time.

She held up her hand. "It's better this way." Angelique returned to her book, staring at the same page she'd been reading and re-reading over the past ten minutes. The pressure of being around him while she kept her secret about Emilee and her non-dead husband was no longer an issue. But what they'd shared—the laughter, the fishing, mostly how wonderfully protected she felt in his arms—that hole was eating her alive.

"So rather than face the music and tell him the truth, you choose instead to avoid him."

"It's worked fairly well so far and more importantly, no one gets hurt." She fought the knot forming in her gut. Deep down she knew her aunt was right.

"I never pegged you for a coward, Angelique."

Her chin quivered, tears threatening her resolve. The truth slashed across her stubborn heart. She was afraid. Afraid of making bad choices again. Dalton was incredible in so many ways—an amazing lover, fun, adventuresome, hardworking, but his temper and drinking reminded her of the very kind of people she'd been running away from all her life. And there was Emilee—she'd die first before she'd allow her to come so close again to being hurt or to grow up in a house where she didn't know how much she was loved. She straightened her shoulders. She couldn't expect her aunt to understand what she'd been through nor did she feel the need to explain. "Once I'm on my feet, Emilee and I will move on. I don't expect you to understand my choices, but I would appreciate your respect of them." She started to walk from the room.

"Angelique."

Her aunt's voice stopped her in her tracks. She waited, studying the small, framed photos hung on the wall going upstairs. Most were of her in various stages of her childhood—one of her blowing out candles on a cake, another of her uncle leading her on her first horse. A more recent one showed a close-up of Emilee and Aunt Rebecca smiling as they held up the first tomato of the season.

"You don't have to let the past define you. But neither should you run from it. All that has happened has helped to make you the woman you are today. You had no power to change your mother, or your ex-husband. You only have the power to change yourself."

"That's exactly what I'm trying to do, Aunt Rebecca," she said, facing her.

Her aunt nodded. "But not all men who get angry are like Tony. Not all people who drink are alcoholic. Have you been truthful with Dalton? Given him the chance to show you the man I believe he is?"

"I know him and his temper, and I know he'll never forgive me for lying to him about Emilee." A trickle of fear curled around her heart. "The Kinnisons are influential around here. What if he fought for custody; what if he tried to take her away from me? I couldn't...I can't even think about that." She shook her head.

"You don't really feel that way."

Angelique released a weary sigh. She'd played the various scenarios over in her mind. In Dalton's eyes, she'd abandoned Emilee once. If he was angry enough with her, why wouldn't he use that against her? "I'm sorry you don't agree with me."

"I'm sorry you seem blind to what is right in front

of you," her aunt fired back. "Dalton cares for you. He would feel the same about Emilee."

"Not if he knew the truth. I can't do that to him. What kind of trust could there ever be between us?"

"I know you're scared. But consider what you may be losing by not trusting Dalton a bit better. You won't know for sure until you tell him the truth."

Angelique dropped her hands to her sides. "Maybe you're right, maybe I'm just a coward."

Her gaze softened. "Not my girl, no. Confused, maybe, but promise me you'll think about it. There are several ways of looking at what seems impossible, Angelique. The best choice isn't always to walk away. Maybe you need to make your head believe what you already know in your heart."

She met her aunt's gaze, brimming with kindness and wisdom. She knew what was coming next.

"You love him."

Chapter Nine

DALTON TOOK A PULL ON the beer he'd been nursing for the past hour. Sitting alone in the backyard, he stared at the tall pine forest beyond the split rail fence, watching the afternoon drift into another sunset. He'd gone on with his life, determined to give Angelique space to figure out whatever the hell she needed to. Maybe he was a fool. Wouldn't be the first time, probably not the last. Closing his eyes, he sighed and let his head drop back against the Adirondack chair. The more he fought how much he missed her, the more the loneliness nibbled away at him.

He heard the mournful sound of an owl, and it seemed to echo in his soul.

"Women are a puzzle."

He responded with a snort. "That's an understatement," he muttered.

"Some are worth it, though, if you're willing to be patient and get all the pieces right."

Dalton sighed. He really didn't need any of Wyatt's sanctimonious mumbo-jumbo right now. "Listen, man, I know you mean well—" He opened one eye and turned to face the voice he'd heard.

And found himself alone.

Slowly he straightened in his chair. He glanced over his shoulder, scanning the dusky shadows. There wasn't a soul in sight.

"Dalton?" Aimee's voice startled him, calling from the deck a good twenty feet from the stone fire pit.

He picked up his beer and, feeling oddly as if a ghost had visited him, walked on unsteady legs back to the house.

"Can you watch Grace for me for a few minutes? I need to check on supper."

"Wyatt's not home?" He gingerly took the baby, cradling the tiny bundle, holding her close, no longer afraid that he might break her.

"He and Rein are with Michael checking on that mare that's about to deliver."

He followed her through the door leading from the deck to the kitchen, his brain scrambling to make sense of what he thought he'd heard. But no one but his brothers knew what he'd been going through, what had had him tied in knots for days.

"Do you feel okay? You look kind of pasty." Her hand paused midair as she looked at him. "You're not coming down with something, are you?"

The scent of the delectable pot roast and potatoes from the oven made his mouth water. "No, I'm good." He glanced out the back door. The fire pit area had been swallowed by the blue-gray evening shadows.

Grace wiggled in his arms and he offered her a finger to play with. She smiled up at him, her blue eyes, so much like her mama's, shining in her cherub face.

"We haven't had a chance to visit in a while. You've been pretty busy with the horses. This is the first time I think you've been up here for supper in the last couple of weeks."

Dalton leaned against the kitchen counter, dividing his attention between the two women in the room, but he couldn't shake the weird feeling that'd he'd just experienced something Michael might refer to as *spirit magic*.

"How are things with you and Angelique?"

Pulled from his thoughts, he blinked. "We're, uh...taking a break. She's been busy. I've been busy." He shrugged.

He caught Aimee's glance as she spooned *au jus* over the roast. "She's been through a lot, I understand."

"Yeah." He made faces at Gracie, battling with her for use of his finger.

"She'll come around. I know you all think women are the complicated ones. But really, we want the same things guys do."

That made him smile. "And what is that, exactly, because that's what I've been trying to figure out for the past two weeks."

Aimee stuck the roast in the oven and swiftly multi-tasked, setting out plates on the counter and warming a bottle before handing it to him along with a burp cloth.

He kicked out a kitchen chair and made himself comfortable while Aimee started putting together a salad.

"Everybody wants to find someone they can trust. Someone who, despite your past, your flaws, loves you anyway. Someone to go through the ups and downs with, right?"

His hungry niece chugged down her bottle with the ease of a seasoned country girl. He tossed the cloth in place and lifted the babe over his shoulder, gently coaxing a surprisingly large burp from her. "That's my girl," he whispered. Glancing up, he found Aimee paused in her task, looking at him with motherly tenderness.

"What? I thought that sounded fantastic."

She smiled. "You're going to make a great dad one day, Dalton Kinnison."

Heat climbed up his neck. He'd heard lots of comments over the years from various people predicting how he'd turn out, but being a good father had never been one of them. He brushed away the odd twist in his chest. "Burping a baby isn't exactly rocket science." He grinned, thinking his pretty sister-in-law was a bit more sappy than usual.

"I've seen you with other kids. Emilee, for one. You're very patient and sweet. She adores you, you can see it." Her eyes welled and she sniffed.

This was veering into territory he didn't know how to handle. "You okay?" He didn't want to appear rude, but this emotional meltdown stuff was not his forte.

She sniffed again and shook her head, returning to chopping peppers for the salad. "I'm just a little emotional these days, I guess. I just wish everyone was as happy as your brother and me." She chopped away as she continued. Dalton couldn't do much else but listen.

"You're such a good guy. I know things haven't been easy for you, but you've managed to overcome so many things in your life. Look at what you guys have done around here—what a legacy Jed has to show for raising you boys. I can't imagine how proud he must be."

Dalton had discovered the root of Wyatt's knew-found sentiment. Still, she was right. Jed had done an amazing job with three very scarred young men, patiently showing them what being a family was all about—showing them what it meant to be a man. Dalton chuckled at the realization dawning in his brain. For too long he'd been clinging to some baseball hat, wishing he knew who his father was, feeling as though he'd been cheated, robbed of a piece of his life. The only one who'd been robbing him was himself.

Gracie had fallen asleep in his arms. Fed. Content. All was right in her little world. "You have an exceptional mama, Gracie June." He handed over the sleeping child and planted a kiss on Aimee's forehead. "Thank you."

She beamed at him, though he swore her eyes were about to leak again. "You're welcome, but I'm not sure what I said that was helpful."

A loud bang of the front door and the sound of boots

hurrying across the wood floor followed. "Miss Aimee! Miss Aimee!" Emilee skidded to a stop, running smack into Dalton. He caught her by the arms and knelt to face her. "What's the matter, Emilee?"

Her eyes, large and brimming with excitement, met his gaze. She could barely hold still long enough to speak. "The mare. She's had her baby colt. It's a boy!" She looked up at Aimee with a wide grin.

Aimee smiled. "Just what we need around here— more boys."

"Hey, now," Dalton shot her a grin.

"Oh, my lord, I never noticed that before." Aimee wore a quizzical expression.

Dalton stood and scooped up Emilee in his arms, giving her a peck on the cheek. It'd been nearly two weeks since Emilee had been allowed to come out to the ranch. He hadn't realized how quiet things had been around here until now. Michael had offered the excuse that her mother and aunt had been keeping her busy with school preparations, but Dalton couldn't help but believe there was more to it than that. It pissed him off at first. He couldn't understand why anything between him and Angelique should have any effect on the friendship he and Emilee had formed over the summer. There again, though, he'd conceded that if Angelique needed time to think things through, he'd give it to her.

"Just a sec, you two. This is such a great picture. Hang on, let me get my phone." Aimee hurried to the dining room to find her purse.

He looked at the little girl and they both shrugged, Emilee collapsing in a fit of giggles that penetrated the sadness in Dalton's heart. "I haven't seen you in a while. You being a good girl and minding your mama?" he asked, searching the little girl's sun-kissed face. Every time he looked at her, he saw Angelique. His heart twisted.

"Yessir. Aunt Rebecca has been making me a bunch of new clothes for third grade. And mama bought me a Hello Kitty backpack."

"Sounds like you're just about ready. Your mama loves you very much," he said, giving her a gentle tug.

Emilee leaned back, her smile fading.

"What is it, punkin'?" He wiggled one of her braids.

"I think my mama misses my daddy."

He searched her eyes and nodded. "Probably so, but what makes you think that?" No, it wasn't his business, and yeah, maybe he was fishing for some shred of sense in what Angelique needed to figure out.

"She doesn't smile much anymore, and she's been working a lot. Grandma says she's trying to save enough so we can have our own house. I want to live on a ranch and raise horses." Her dark eyes twinkled when she looked at him.

"Here we go. Now big smiles, both of you," Aimee said, holding the camera steady.

Dalton smiled cheek-to-cheek with the little girl. "Cheese," they said in unison.

"You want to come down and see the new colt?" Emilee wiggled free of his grasp and grabbed his hand.

"Sure, I do." He looked at Aimee, who held Gracie cradled in one arm, her free hand holding the phone up as she studied it. Dalton tapped Emilee's nose. "You go on down. I'll be there in a few minutes. I want to make sure Miss Aimee doesn't need my help anymore, okay punkin'?"

She giggled. "It's funny when you call me punkin'." She turned on her little cowboy boot heel and took off as fast as she'd arrived.

"Don't run in the house," he called just for good measure, as it fell on deaf ears anyway.

"You need me to put Gracie in her crib before I go?"

Aimee focused on the phone. "What? Oh, no, I'll take care of it."

Puzzled as to why she insisted on taking the photo, he walked over to her. He peered at the picture. "Did it come out all right?"

The image hit him with the force of a moving train. He blinked and tipped Aimee's hand to see it at a better angle. He couldn't look away. He glanced up and met her curious look. Was it possible? No one knew about that night nearly seven years ago. Dalton's gaze shot back to the picture. It was either totally uncanny or…*holy crap.*

"Dalton?"

He heard Aimee's voice, but his brain felt on overload, blocking the sound. All this time, pretending to care about him and yet holding him at arm's length, talking about the things she'd done, the choices she'd made. The lies….

To her daughter.

To those around her.

To him.

God, he felt like a fool. "Jesus." He shook his head. It was enough to deal with the fact that she'd lied to him and a kick in the gut to know his own daughter had been right under his nose all this time. He squeezed his eyes and swiped his hand over his mouth. "You see it, don't you?"

"I don't know why I hadn't until now. I hadn't really ever seen the two of you together—"

"She lied to me." His eyes searched Aimee's hoping for her to say something that would make sense of this. "Jesus, Aimee, all this time, why would she do that?" Pain twisted his heart.

"Dalton," she said. "You need to slow down. Yes, from that angle, with you both smiling like that, it's remarkable, I agree. But we don't know for sure until you speak with Angelique."

He listened, confused, bewildered, feeling betrayed. "Did you mean what you said about me making a good father one day?" He had to hear it again. Had to make himself believe that despite Angelique apparently not seeing him as a long-term commitment or a good father, someone *did*.

"Oh, Dalton, of course. If you find out without a doubt—"

He knew. It was as though a light shone in his brain, making everything clear. Maybe he'd always known but was too willing to concede that Angelique didn't find him fit for much else than a temporary good time. He took a deep breath. She had another thing coming. If she wouldn't tell him the truth, there were such things as blood tests that would solve this question. She'd lied to the wrong person and, by damn, he was going to get some answers. "I've got to go.

"Please, give her a chance to explain." Aimee touched his arm. "We don't know everything she's been through."

He swallowed hard, tamping down his need to throw something. "Okay," he said more to himself than to his sister-in-law. "I need some answers, Aimee. I've been straight with her about how I feel. I deserve to know if this is why she keeps pushing me away."

She nodded. "Call if you need anything."

He nodded and took out his phone. "Can you send that photo to my phone?"

She nodded, quickly making the transfer. He waited to be sure it came through. "Thanks."

He hurried out to his truck, pausing long enough to see the light pouring out of the barn. Though he had no proof other than a single photo of the child whose smile resembled his, he couldn't help but wonder if Michael and Rebecca had known that she was his when they brought Emilee to End of the Line.

He glanced at the clock in his truck. It was a little after six p.m. Angelique should be home, or would be very soon. This time she wasn't going to get rid of him so easily, not at least until he heard the truth from her lips.

A few moments later, he pulled into the gravel drive of the Greyfeather farm. The front door was open, allowing the evening breeze through the screen door. Angelique's car wasn't in sight. He shut off the ignition, deciding that he could find out whether Rebecca, too, had been keeping Angelique's secret.

Rebecca appeared at the screen door as he walked up the steps.

"Dalton."

"Rebecca," he replied.

"Angelique's not home yet from work."

"That's fine. I'll start with you, then."

She searched his face and, with a nod, opened the door to invite him in. "I've been expecting you to pay a visit."

He glanced at her. "You have?"

"The sight," she commented quietly.

"Oh." He nodded, unable to keep the sarcasm at bay. "Handy thing to have at your disposal, I imagine." He stood in the narrow foyer. The house, a simple three-story clapboard, felt like a dollhouse in comparison to the vaulted ceilings and expansive rooms he was used to at the ranch.

"Please, come in." She ushered him to one of the love seats covered in traditional American Indian design. The room was comfortable, tailor-made for the salt-of the-earth folks he'd always known them to be. "I'll get us something to drink—lemonade, tea?"

He shook his head no. Seated on the edge of the couch, he folded his hands over his knees. "No, I'm good, thank you." Which was a lie. He was nowhere near good and his system craved either so long as it was laced liberally with Jack Daniels—which was part of why he was here. He waited, staring at the floor, searching for how to begin.

She sat in the rocking chair across from him, one of Rein's handmade tree-trunk coffee tables between them. Scattered across its top were papers with sketches of horses that Emilee had been working on.

"She's got a wonderful, creative mind," Rebecca said as though reading his mind. "Just like Angelique, when she was young—always drawing animals."

Dalton glanced up at the woman, seemingly lost in her thoughts. "I don't know exactly how to ask this, and to be honest, I'm not entirely sure I'm ready to hear the truth, but I feel I deserve to hear it, either way." He pulled out his phone and handed it to her. "Aimee took this just a short time ago, back at the ranch."

The older woman held it carefully, showing no emotion, no reaction at all.

"Do you notice anything?" he asked.

She handed the phone back. "I encouraged her to tell you."

There it was. Emilee *was* his daughter—his own flesh and blood. He raised his brows, the force of her comment like a sucker punch. He stared at her, letting his brain absorb the truth. "Then *you knew?*" he asked, trying to remain calm. How many people knew about this other than the one person who *should*?

"Only for certain the day of the barbecue. I had hoped that she would have used the privacy you had at the cabin to explain everything."

He thought back to the twenty-four hours they'd spent together in seclusion. While she'd mentioned a couple of times that she'd had some difficulties, it seemed she hadn't wanted to think about them. So, he hadn't pushed her. Instead, he'd allowed attraction to outweigh intelligence. Reasoning that the more time they spent together, the more she'd be able to trust him…ironically. "Why wouldn't she tell me? Why'd I have to find out like this? As if it didn't matter—as if *I* don't matter." I have a little girl who's almost seven—*seven*." He tried to understand, but just couldn't. He looked at Rebecca. "I've missed out on seven years."

Rebecca's soft, motherly gaze searched his. "When she called us to come get Emilee, we had no idea. You must believe me."

He dug his palms into his forehead. His brain was a mess…his life, suddenly a fucking train wreck. "Does she think so little of me? Think that I wouldn't care, or be a good father to Emilee?" God, the woman had taken his heart on some wild roller-coaster ride these past few weeks. Knowing the thrill of her body next to his, the serenity of watching her sleep, hearing her laughter and being damn giddy thinking he'd caused it. He swiped his hands down over his face. "I don't understand why she didn't contact me when she found out."

"You were both very different people back then. I feel Angelique should be the one to explain everything, but I can tell you that she did not know for certain who Emilee's father was until after she was born. By then, she'd married, and I think she'd hoped the baby would help save the marriage. She didn't want your life to be changed—you never wanted family—you'd made that clear to her."

He shook his head. "You know what's funny? I should've never let her get out of that truck that night. I should have asked her to stay, not let her go back to Chicago. Maybe I was scared." He looked at Rebecca. "Maybe I didn't want to face what I felt back then. Maybe I figured that she had what she wanted waiting for her." He swallowed, picked up his phone, and stared at the photo. In every other way—her hair, her mannerisms, her love for horses—he'd only seen Angelique. In these past few weeks, he'd grown accustomed to seeing Emilee running around the ranch. Before that, their lives had barely crossed. Still, it wasn't until Angelique returned to End of the Line that Dalton begin to change his mind about second chances, starting over. He held out his hand, surrendering to what he knew of himself back then and what he'd come to realize in a few short weeks. "You're right. She was right. I didn't want the same things that my brothers did. I thought having my freedom to do whatever I pleased was enough." He shrugged. "I thought I'd be content to be single for a long time—if not for the rest of my life."

"As long as you were the one calling the shots, deciding when the relationship was over, you couldn't get hurt. The same as you'd seen Jed get hurt, the same hurt you felt when your mom left you boys." She walked around the table and sat beside him. She put a hand on his arm.

He shook his head. "Yeah, maybe."

"Angelique was afraid, Dalton. She can go into detail if she chooses, but her ex-husband was abusive, both physically and mentally. It's taken her a long time, and it may take the rest of her life to fully recover. But I know she's determined to stand on her own and take care of the one person she loves more than her own life—Emilee. Her little girl. *Your* little girl."

"I love her, Rebecca." He looked up at her. "I'm in love with her."

She smiled. "I know and deep down, I think she knows you do. But her past, a dangerous, frightening part of her life, is still very real."

He wasn't sure what the older woman meant. "You

mean the things that her husband put her though, the one who died overseas? How could he be a threat to her now?"

Rebecca held his gaze and released a sigh. Dalton braced himself.

"They are divorced, it's true, but for her and Emilee's safety, no one but her lawyer knows she's here."

Confused, Dalton tried to make sense of this new information. "I don't understand."

Rebecca paused a moment as though debating whether to say any more.

"Rebecca, I've just found out I have a seven-year-old daughter. How bad can it be?"

"She was key witness in testifying against her husband on a variety of charges— manslaughter, drug-trafficking, I don't know what else—anyway, she managed to divorce him and she has a no-contact order in place should he ever receive an early parole."

Dalton stared at the woman. He'd already ascertained that the man was no hero as she'd made everyone think, but he was having trouble wrapping his brain around this new information. "Any man who abuses a woman is no hero in my book—I don't care if he's a five-star general. That much I figured out. But you're telling me this bastard is still alive?"

"He was in the service and at first she thought his anger issues were primarily related to his post stress. But things got progressively worse. Counseling didn't help, but knowing my niece's tenacity, she probably felt she had enough stamina, enough faith and love to weather them through."

She stood and walked over to the front window, briefly lifting the curtain. She wore a worried look. "She learned the hard way that you can't change another person." Rebecca faced him. "You can only change yourself."

Dalton dropped back in the chair, the news blind-siding him. He sat for a moment, letting the pieces fall together. As unexpected, as frustrating as it was to hear it all, it nonetheless began to make sense. The only thing he didn't know for sure was how Angelique felt about him. He stood, restless in his need to talk to her. He checked the time, noting it was almost seven.

Rebecca crossed over to where her phone lay under a bolt of material. "This isn't like her to not call when she's going to be late. Though she did mention she had to close tonight with her boss leaving early."

A gasp from Rebecca pulled Daltons gaze to hers.

"There's a missed call from Angelique's lawyer. He's been trying to reach her all afternoon."

"About what?"

She looked up. "Apparently Tony walked away from a work house this morning and remains at large."

"Does he know she lived here? Did he know where you lived?"

She shook her head. "We never met him. I don't think Angelique would have sent Emilee here if she'd ever mentioned living in End of the Line.

He dialed Angelique's number. It went straight to voicemail. "Voicemail." He glanced at Rebecca. "Would she shut off her phone?"

Rebecca shook her head.

"Okay, I'm heading down to Billings. Call Michael, but don't alarm Emilee." He headed to his truck, letting the screen door slam behind him.

"Be careful, Dalton," Rebecca called after him.

"Keep calling her number. If you don't get an answer in the next ten minutes, call the Billings police and send them over." He had no Crow, no Choctaw blood in him that he knew of, but something caused Dalton's gut to twist in a knot. He punched her number once more and it leapt to her voicemail. "Dammit," he muttered, tossing the phone on the seat and pressing his foot down on the gas pedal.

Exhausted from a long week, Angelique gathered up the towels she'd used to bathe the dogs kenneled for the weekend. Dr. Benson had taken off early to go fishing and the fact that he trusted her to close up boosted her spirits. He'd been talking about taking more time off, if she thought she could handle things with his permanent staff.

"Don't you look damn sexy in those scrubs," a low-timbered voice said.

She dropped the wet towels in the basket and lifted it, prepared to tell Dalton that she hadn't changed her mind. Her heart stopped.

With nothing but the counter between them stood Tony, dressed in dirty jeans and a too small T-shirt. A beard, new since she'd last seen him, covered the bottom half of his face. All she could think was that her lawyer was supposed to have contacted her if he'd gotten an early release. Angelique doubted very much that the Illinois correctional facility even knew where Tony was.

She reached for her phone, and he leapt over the counter and plucked it out of her hand. He then ripped the landline phone off the wall and threw it across the room.

Angelique gripped the basket, her eyes on his. "What are you doing here?" She glanced at the exit sign at the end of the hallway to the alley.

He sauntered toward her. His eyes were bloodshot, rimmed with dark circles, his smile menacing. "Is that any way to talk to your husband?"

She adjusted the basket, prepared to throw it at him if necessary. "That's ex-husband, and you're under a no–contact order."

He shrugged. "Had to see my girl."

She swallowed hard, the fear climbing in her throat. There was little traffic after five in this part of town. "My uncle is expecting me to help him; he'll suspect something is wrong if I don't show up at a specific time." She hoped the fact that she'd not gotten around to calling Aunt Rebecca to tell her she'd be running later than normal would make her curious.

Tony glanced at the phone, looked at her, and then threw it against the wall. It splintered into pieces, scattering across the tile floor.

She wouldn't be a victim. Hugging the basket, she ran at him, ramming him backwards with everything she had. His body slammed up against the plate glass window, cracking it from top to bottom. Taking advantage of his dazed state, she dropped the basket and ran down the back hall, pushing open the exit door. She stumbled into the alley, searching for someone nearby.

"You can't run from me, bitch! You'll pay for what you did to me!" he yelled.

She bolted for the front parking lot. If she could get to her car, there was an extra key hidden in the console. She heard the crunch of gravel from his rapid footsteps as she tried to open the driver's side door. Her head snapped back and she cried out. He wrapped her braid around his fist, pulling her away from the car, his mouth pressed against her ear.

"I told you I'd find you. I've had plenty of time to think about what I'm going to do to you."

Tears squeezed past her eyes. Thoughts of never seeing Emilee again, of never having the chance to tell Dalton about Emilee, to hope he could forgive her. She fought against his grip, unwilling to give up. "You won't do this to me again," she yelled, bringing her boot heel-down hard on the top of his foot.

His grip loosened, but before she could turn to jab his eyes, he regained control and slammed her face against the back end of the car. Her teeth felt jarred loose and she saw spots, but she knew if she blacked out now she'd have no chance of survival. She summoned everything inside, turning and twisting until she could stab her fingertips into his eyes.

"You crazy bitch!" he screamed, and she felt his iron fist pound more than once into her ribs.

Doubled over, she fought to breathe. Another blow came, across her back this time. She dropped to her knees.

"You stupid bitch, did you really think you could go hand-to-hand with me?"

The toe of his boot slammed into her side and she felt her rib snap. Her breath came in short gasps as she tried curl herself into a ball and protect her side from the repeated blows. He grabbed her shoulder and tossed her to her back. Unable to move, she lay there, her face swollen, barely able to see. He stood over her. The streetlight glinted off the silver blade in his hand.

"It'll look like a robbery. You stupidly tried to stop it and the unfortunate happened." His voice was cold, calculating.

"Please don't. Think of Emilee…our child." It was all she had left. Tears streamed down her cheeks.

He squatted down beside her, his eyes full of hatred. "Emilee's not mine, and for that I'm damn grateful. I never wanted kids and especially not with you. Did I forget to mention I was sterile?"

Bile rose in her throat. "Then why? Why'd you stay?" she asked. Her face throbbed; she tasted the tang of blood on her split lip.

He twisted the tip of the knife against his forefinger, holding it just above her face. "I needed a cover, sweetheart. Someone who'd play the part of the good wife, not ask questions. You were so damn hopeful that you could change me. It worked like a charm, until you started listening to that nosy ass neighbor of yours."

"Ellie? God, no, tell me you didn't hurt her." She winced at her pain, ached for her friend, the one who'd helped her through everything.

"Needed a car when I got out. Let's just say she wasn't very compliant." Tony grinned.

How had she been so blind not to see this monster behind her husband's face?

"You don't have to do this," she pleaded, trying to inch away. She closed her fist around a small pile of gravel. He snorted as he grabbed her by the front of her shirt and hauled her to her feet. He brought her face close to his.

"Paybacks are hell, sweetheart."

She tossed the gravel in his face and, at the same time, felt a searing pain in her lower left side. Then there came a roar, almost deafening, followed by the sound of tires on gravel. She didn't know what happened, where Tony had gone. Her body gave out and she slid to the ground, glad for the chance to close her eyes.

"Angel, no! No, sweetheart, you stay with me," the frantic voice urged. "Help is on the way. Godammit, stay awake." Something was patting her cheek. She shook her head. It hurt. She wanted to rest, if she could just rest. Through a blurred haze of exhaustion and pain, she saw Dalton's face leaning down, cradling her head in his lap. She tried to smile. "Dalton."

"Ssshh, save your strength." She winced as he applied pressure to the throbbing pain in her side.

"It was Tony. My ex-husband...Tony." She grabbed his wrist, fighting to stay awake. She needed to tell him. She didn't want him to find out from someone else if she didn't make it. "There's something I need to tell you," she forced through the pain. Every breath grew more difficult, draining her energy.

"You can tell me later, Angel." He stroked her cheek.

She shook her head. "No, if I—Dalton, it's Emilee. She's yours." Tears leaked from her eyes, stinging her wounds. "That night—"

She saw the painful truth crumple his face. The sound of sirens grew close. "I'm so...sorry." She just needed to rest, just for a moment.

"Don't you leave me, Angel. Not now. Not when we've just found each other again. I know, baby. I know Emilee is mine. Stay with me. Come on, stay, Angel."

She felt the warmth of a bright light, but was jostled from it by someone shaking her shoulder.

"Stay with me," she heard the voice say.

"I see Jed," she whispered, and the world went black.

Chapter Ten

DALTON STARED AT THE BOTTLE. He hadn't opened it. He was scared to, afraid if he did, he wouldn't be able to stop. He'd already gotten more than a couple of odd looks from patrons seated in the dive bar not more than a block from the hospital. Rancid stale smoke and booze permeated the wood and ancient ceiling above. But it was dark, quiet, and no one bothered him. And that's exactly what he needed, except for maybe this bottle of Jack Daniels. He picked up the empty glass, still sparkling clean from the dishwasher.

"Hey, mind if I join you?"

He looked up and met Rein's curious gaze. Curious for the same reason everyone else in the place was curious. Was he going to crack that bottle and pour himself a drink? He'd been staring at the damn thing for nearly an hour debating the same thing.

"Suit yourself; bartender's a pretty nice guy," Dalton replied. He held the glass in his hand, turning it slowly, watching the dim light glint off its surface. "You know, I've been sitting here" —he glanced at his brother—"thinking about drinking this. How good it would taste, how it'd make the pain go away. Then I thought, maybe if I made a pact with God, maybe if I swore off drinking for good, maybe he'd let her live."

Rein ordered himself a soda, stopped the waitress, and made it two. He took off his hat and laid it in the seat beside him. "There's no news yet. She's still in surgery. How are you holding up?"

He shrugged. "I couldn't stand that waiting room any longer." His brain had gone on autopilot when he'd heard that she needed emergency surgery to repair her kidney. He couldn't think about it, didn't want to think about the possibility of losing her. He shook his head, not allowing his thoughts to travel that road. "Did Michael and Rebecca make it?"

Rein nodded. "Just after you left. Wyatt stayed back with Aimee and the ranch."

"And Emilee?"

"With her grandparents."

It was awkward, him knowing that he was her father and her not aware of it. The kid still thought her dad was buried in Arlington Cemetery.

"She's okay, Dalton. She's a tough little kid." Rein held his gaze.

"So, Aimee told you about the picture?"

Rein sighed. "Yeah, did you find out anything?"

Dalton's mouth curled. "Yeah, I'm her dad."

Rein leaned back in his seat. "That must have come as quite a shock."

Dalton picked up the bottle and studied the smallest wording on the label. "You've no idea."

"And Emilee doesn't know?"

Dalton shook his head. "I just hope that when she gets through this, Angelique is going to want to tell her the truth." He swallowed the fresh lump of pain that surfaced unexpectedly.

"Hey." Rein leaned his elbows on the table. "It's going to be okay. Everything is going to work out, you'll see."

Dalton rubbed his eyelids. His eyes were weary, bloodshot probably from the dam that had broken finally inside him. He had watched—his shirt covered in her blood—as they took her from him on the gurney, wheeling her into a fray of physicians barking out orders.

He'd searched the halls for a restroom and, finding one in a secluded hall, went in, locked the door, and wept. Years of anger and bitterness toward his mom, regret for not appreciating Jed more, for not being there when Emilee was born, for not saving Angelique from the pain, she'd endured being married to that bastard.

"I understand that they caught the piece of shit who did this. Hiding out in a dumpster a couple of blocks away. Guess they followed a trail of blood."

Dalton found some satisfaction in that. "She wouldn't have gone down without a fight. Not my Angel." He looked at Rein. "He better pray they put him away for good, because I'll be waiting for him next time."

Rein finished one soda and offered a last chance to Dalton for the other. "I doubt you'll have to worry about a next time. Attempted murder, along with premeditation, puts him in a new wing at the hotel."

Dalton released a heavy sigh. He pushed the unopened whiskey bottle aside. "You know, it's the oddest damn thing. I came in here desperate for a drink, but the truth is I don't have the stomach for it. I don't want it, don't need it. I don't know, maybe the desire will come back, maybe it won't. All I know is that I want to be able to tell her I don't need it like I did. She and Emilee, that's what I want. That's all I need."

Rein nodded. "And you'll get the chance to tell her, Dalton. I know you will." An old-fashioned ringtone sounded in Rein's shirt pocket.

Dalton studied his brother's face as he listened to the caller.

"Okay, we'll be right over. I love you too, baby." Rein tucked his phone away. "She's on her way up to ICU." He fished in his pocket and dropped a five on the table.

Dalton was waiting at the door before Rein could put his hat back on.

What was but a few moments seemed like an eternity as Dalton waited for Michael, Rebecca, and Emilee to spend a moment or two with Angelique. She was out still from the anesthesia, but they'd allowed her family to see her. Emilee and her grandmother stood beside the bed as Michael recited a prayer over his niece's battered body.

Rebecca touched Dalton's arm as they left the room. "Talk to her, let her know you're here. It will help."

He glanced at Emilee and she ran to him, wrapping her arms around his waist, holding on with a fierce grip. He swallowed hard and bent down to look at her. "We must be brave, Em. She needs our strength to get better."

Emilee nodded, then leaned forward and hugged his neck. "I love you, Dalton."

Daltons raised his eyes and met Rebecca's shimmering gaze. He cleared his throat. "I love you too, Em. We're going to get through this, all of us are. You go with your grandma now. I want to go see your mom."

She stepped out of his embrace and turned quickly back. "Be sure to tell her that you love her, too."

Dalton's eyes watered. "I will, Em." He nodded.

Swiping his hand across his eyes, he watched the pair walk down the hall. A nurse leaving the room nearly ran into him.

"Are you family?" she asked.

"Uh, yes, fiancé." It wasn't a total lie, just not quite a reality yet.

"Just for a few moments," she told him. "She needs to rest."

Dalton nodded and stepped into the semi–dark room. Intubated, she lay still, her head bandaged, face purpled from her injuries. He lifted her hand and silently willed every ounce of strength he had inside him to her. "I want you to know that Emilee is fine. She's holding up really good. She's got a strong will like her mama." He looked toward the ceiling to summon his strength. Releasing a quiet sigh, he searched her face again. "I don't know if you can hear me, Angel. But you need to come back to us, darlin.' Emilee, your uncle and aunt—everyone— needs you. I need you." He swallowed, reaffirming his resolve. "I know you think that things are too messed up to make it right, but they aren't. Someone once told me that the things that matter, even if the pieces are scattered, are worth having if you have the patience to put it back together."

He pulled up a chair close to her bed, and kissed her hand. "I love you and I want us—you, me, and Emilee— to be a family, a real family. And hell, I don't know, maybe you'll decide you want more kids and that's okay by me." He watched and waited for some sign that she'd heard him. The steady blip of her heart monitor was his only reassurance that she was still alive. "I'm sorry I haven't been there for you. I'm sorry that my drinking kept you from seeing the man I truly am. And I hope you can see it in your heart to give me a chance to be a good dad to Em, a good husband for you."

A loud buzz echoed in the room and several nurses invaded the space. "I'm sorry, you'll have to leave now."

Dalton was moved aside as several medical staff swallowed Angelique from his view. He felt as though his heart had stopped as he watched them prepare the paddles.

"Sir, you have to leave." One of the nurses took him by the arm and gently led him into the hall.

"Is she—?" He couldn't bring himself to say the word.

"We're doing all we can, sir. Please, wait down the hall with the others."

And she was gone. He stared at the closed blinds that cut off his view of what was happening inside.

"Dalton Kinnison?" A grim-faced nurse stood at the doorway of the packed waiting room, scanning the more than two dozen family and friends from End of the Line. All waiting on word about Angelique.

Dalton pushed to his feet. "That's me." Confused, he glanced at Rebecca and Michael.

"Please, come with me."

Dalton's heart thrummed in his chest. It'd been more than an hour, maybe two, since they'd run him out of the room. He followed the nurse down the hall and arrived as one of the doctors was leaving Angelique's room. "Is she going to be okay, doc?" He hadn't realized he was clutching the poor man's arm until the kind physician covered his hand and patted it.

"She's had a little setback. Nothing we'd consider serious, however with this type of surgery the body has to reset itself. The next forty-eight hours will be the most crucial for her and the baby."

Dalton's brain stopped. *Baby?* "I'm sorry, did you say baby?"

The doctor, busy with signing off on a chart, was oblivious that he'd just sent Dalton's world into a tailspin. "Yes, Mr. Kinnison. She was awake for a few moments before surgery and insisted that you should know, regardless of what happens."

Dalton's hand fell away, his arm limp. He backed up and leaned against the wall. *Baby?* He felt a tug on his hand and looked down to find Emilee holding it.

"It's going to be okay, Mr. Kinnison. My grandma said so."

He knelt and drew the young girl into his arms, holding her tightly, unaware until this moment how amazing it felt to hug your child.

She leaned back then, studying him with eyes that were wise beyond her years. "You're my father, aren't you?"

Another hit to the solar plexus. He blinked and swallowed the sudden lump in his throat. 'Did your mom tell you that?"

She shook her head.

"Your grandma?"

A shy smile curved her lips. "I asked to see the picture that Miss Aimee took of us. It's a pretty remarkable likeness."

Tears stung at the back of his eyes. He swiped them and forced a smile, trying to keep his composure. "What would you think about that?" He sniffed. *Jesus*. Angelique had to make it. He covered his mouth, pushing away any thoughts to the contrary.

Emilee wrapped her fingers around his hand. "I think my mom needs you, and I think I need my daddy—my real daddy. And my little brother is going to need his daddy, too."

Her smile lifted his heart, making him think damn near anything was possible. "Who told you…?"

She raised her tiny brow.

"Right," he said with a smile. Dalton stood and took Emilee's hand in his. He faced the doctor. "Can I take my daughter in to see her mother?"

The older man nodded as he brushed his hand over Emilee's head. "She's awake, but she needs her rest. You two keep it short."

Epilogue

ANGELIQUE SCANNED THE TABLE, LOOKING at those seated around it. Here was her family, the family she'd always dreamt of having, the people who would be there to help and support, love and laugh with her. Ellie, who's violent encounter with Tony helped to solidify Tony's permanent residence. Angelique was grateful for all she'd done in the past and eventually talked the woman into moving End of the Line, where she'd shortly thereafter taken a position as head of a safe house for women and children in Billings. Angelique's heart swelled with gratitude. Here were her aunt and uncle, Sally, and Betty—people she'd known since she was a young girl. She wanted Emilee to know that familiarity, for her and Dalton and the new family they'd started to have it also.

It was surreal to think how life can change in a moment. They'd told her that in post-op recovery that her heart had faltered. She'd been able to hear everything Dalton had said. Heard the plea in his voice, telling her that he loved her, he loved Emilee. She wanted to respond—tried too—but couldn't.

Her body, her heart responded instead and that was when she found herself alone in a white fog, much like a misty spring morning in the mountains. There she'd seen Jed. He told her she couldn't stay, that she had a family to raise. She needed to watch out for his son, that he was some of his best work.

Later, when she'd told Dalton, she feared he might find the story odd. Instead, he'd looked at her and smiled, seemingly not at all surprised. "You ought to talk more to your uncle about this. I think there is some truth in this stuff he believes in. I didn't used to put much stock into it, but I want to know more. I want Emilee to understand her heritage better." The moment had changed her in ways unimaginable, grounding her, giving her peace.

"Do you need anything else?"

She looked up to accept the water refill and smiled. "I'm good." She met Dalton's mouth in a tender kiss and then patted her belly. "I've been eating all day."

Pride and more love than she dared to hope possible shimmered in his dark eyes. He leaned down and whispered in her ear. "You know, our daughter claims she's going to have a little brother."

Angelique looked across the table to where Emilee was busy showing Ellie sketches of the new colt, now three months old and as feisty as his little human admirer. It seemed the two had bonded and that's where she spent her every moment after school.

Dalton sat down next to her and leaned over to kiss her once more. There'd been much of that, as well as a civil ceremony at Dalton's insistence once she'd been released from the hospital. Already the paperwork had been started to correct Emilee's birth certificate, naming both Dalton and Angelique as her legal parents. But he'd promised a celebration later at the ranch, because, as he'd told her, "Those sisters-in-law of mine won't have it any other way."

Angelique looked around, unable to count the number of ways she was blessed on this Thanksgiving Day.

Liberty stood at her place as the last platter of food was placed on the table that Rein had custom made for Kinnison family celebrations. The array of food was good enough for a king's royal feast. "Since this is my new home, I'd like to offer a toast—first, to my amazing husband, his brothers and friends one and all, who helped get this house built and ready in time for our first family celebration. To Jed for creating a legacy that will carry on in our children and our children's children. To my sisters—we're outlaws and I love you more than you'll ever know." She stopped and smiled as everyone, glasses raised, waited for her to finish. "And to family, those by blood and those by choice, and to those yet to join us." She glanced at Angelique, and then directed her grin toward Rein as she touched her belly.

Emilee squealed, the first to show she understood what Liberty had implied. Rein's eyes widened and he stood, grabbing her in bear hug as everyone applauded. The sumptuous meal was delayed by a flurry of hugs and congratulations.

Rein grabbed his glass as everyone made their way back to their seats. "To the Kinnison legacy!"

"To the Kinnsion legacy," they all responded in unison.

DEAR READERS,
 I hope you enjoyed reading Dalton and Angelique's story. Dalton was one of my favorite Kinnison brothers to write about. He'd been carrying around his anger and bitterness of his mom's abandonment for years, brooding inwardly that he never knew who his father was. To see the change when he finally does realize who that is, is a pivotal turning point in his attitude. But ahead lies a great many more obstacles that he must face. That's what I love most about writing romance. Watching my characters go through some tough times, and yet, somehow, through it all, love finds a way.

I invite you to read the other two books so far in this series of the formidable Kinnison men and the women who tame them! Here is a bit about RUGGED HEARTS, Book I (Wyatt & Aimee's story) and RUSTLER'S HEART, Book II (Rein & Liberty's story.) Each is stand alone, but the town, the family and secondary characters blend into a rich tapestry of community, hope, second chances, and lots of romance! (Of course!)

~ Amanda

Other Books by
Amanda McIntyre

NON-FICTION:
A Taste of Gratitude & Joy (w/CH Admirand)
Crumbs in the Keyboard (w/Sheryl Hames Torres)

CONTEMPORARY WESTERN ROMANCE:
KINNISON LEGACY:
Rugged Hearts
Rustler's Heart
Renegade Hearts
All I Want for Christmas

LAST HOPE RANCH:
Mr. December
No Strings Attached
Worth the Wait

END OF THE LINE, MONTANA:
Lost and Found
Georgia on My Mind
Hurricane Season

CONTEMPORARY ROMANCE:
Thunderstruck
Stranger in Paradise
Tides of Autumn
Unfinished Dreams
Wish You Were Here

HISTORICAL:
A Warrior's Heart
The Promise
Closer to You (formerly Wild & Unruly)
Christmas Angel (formerly Fallen Angel)
Tirnan 'Oge
When Candy Met Cupid
The Dark Seduction of Miss Jane

HARLEQUIN SPICE/HISTORICAL:
The Master & the Muses
★(audio/international)

The Diary of Cozette
★(audio/international)

Tortured
★(audio/international)

The Pleasure Garden
★(audio/international)

Winter's Desire
★(audio/international)

Dark Pleasures
★(audio/international)

About the Author

Published internationally in print, eBook, and Audio, bestselling author Amanda McIntyre finds inspiration from the American Heartland that she calls home. Best known for her Kinnison Legacy cowboys and Last Hope Ranch series, her passion is writing emotional, character-driven small town contemporary western, historical, women's fiction, and Celtic fantasy. Amanda truly believes that no matter what, love will always find a way.

Find out more about Amanda's books:

Website: http://www.amandamcintyresbooks.com
Newsletter: http://bit.ly/AtHeartNewsletter
Book Bub: http://bit.ly/AmandasBookbubPage
Facebook: https://www.facebook.com/AmandaMcIntyreAuthorPage
All Author: https://allauthor.com/author/amandaauthor/
TWITTER: https://twitter.com/amandamcintyre1

Made in the USA
Coppell, TX
25 June 2022

79254646R00104